「NEW TOEIC 常考字彙」全部取材自新的 TOEIC 全真試題，等於把試題中的單字挖出來給你背，背完後，考試立刻輕鬆。

　　背單字是學英文的第一步。這本手冊同學可以放在身上，隨時隨地背，每天背單字可以消除煩惱。背英文單字千萬不要死記，死背會忘記。較難的單字我們都有字根分析，同學可以舉一反三。

　　TOEIC 成績是國際英語能力證明的依據。利用 TOEIC 考高分的目標，順道把英文學好，一舉兩得。

　　本書雖經過多次審慎校對，仍恐有疏漏之處，尚祈各界先進不吝批評指正。

劉 毅

A a

abdomen 〔'æbdəmən 〕 *n.* 腹部

Some people call the *abdomen* their tummy or stomach.

【abdomen = belly】

abolish 〔 ə'balɪʃ 〕 *v.* 廢除

The president decided to *abolish* the unreasonable rules.

abreast 〔 ə'brɛst 〕 *adv.* 並肩地

Anna and Rita walked to school two *abreast*. 【abreast = a + breast（胸部）】

abrupt 〔 ə'brʌpt 〕 *adj.* 突然的

I enjoyed the book except for its *abrupt* ending.

ab + rupt
| |
off + break

absence 〔'æbsn̩s 〕 *n.* 缺席

Jack could not explain his *absence* from class. 【相反詞是 presence 〔'prɛzn̩s 〕 *n.* 出席】

abundant ﹝ ə'bʌndənt ﹞ *adj.* 豐富的

Oil is *abundant* in this area.

access ﹝'æksɛs ﹞ *n.* 通路;接近或使用權

The dirt road provides the
only *access* to the house.

ac	+	cess
to	+	go

acclaim ﹝ ə'klem ﹞ *v.* 稱讚

The journalist was *acclaimed*
for his courage in reporting
the truth.

ac	+	claim
to	+	cry

accompany ﹝ ə'kʌmpənɪ ﹞ *v.* 陪伴

My sister asked me to *accompany* her to
the store.【去當 company (同伴),即「陪伴」】

accomplish ﹝ ə'kɑmplɪʃ ﹞ *v.* 完成

The task will not be *accomplished* in a
few days.

accordance 〔 ə'kɔrdṇs 〕 *n.* 一致；
符合

In *accordance* with the rules, we speak
softly. 【*in accordance with* 依照】

accordingly 〔 ə'kɔrdɪŋlɪ 〕 *adv.* 因此

He had loved her and he had been,
accordingly, good to her.

【 accordingly = therefore = consequently 】

accountant 〔 ə'kauntənt 〕 *n.* 會計師

The *accountant* was accused of cooking
the books in order to
help his client avoid
paying taxes.

ac +	count +	ant
to +	計算 +	人

accrue 〔 ə'kru 〕 *v.* 孳生（利息）；增加

My savings have been
accruing interest for the
last ten years.

ac +	crue
to +	*grow*

accurate 〔'ækjərɪt 〕 *adj.* 精確的

His *accurate* prediction
saved many people's
lives and property.

ac	+ cur	+ ate
to	+ care	+ adj.

【accurate = correct = exact】

accustomed 〔ə'kʌstəmd 〕 *adj.* 習慣的

I have lived near the railway for so long
now that I've grown *accustomed* to the
noise.【先背 custom ('kʌstəm) *n.* 習俗】

achieve 〔ə'tʃiv 〕 *v.* 達成

In order to *achieve* your goal you must
work hard.【名詞是 achievements (成就)】

acknowledge 〔ək'nɑlɪdʒ 〕 *v.* 承認

I have to *acknowledge* that Harry is
smarter than my brother.

【acknowledge = ac + knowledge (知識)】

A

acutely ﹝ ə'kjutlɪ ﹞ *adv.* 劇烈地

Tina's arm hurt *acutely* after she twisted it.【先背 cute (可愛的)，一點也不可愛的變化，表示「劇烈地」】

adapt ﹝ ə'dæpt ﹞ *v.* 適應

The southerners found it difficult to *adapt* to the cold weather.

【adapt (適應)、adept (熟練的)、adopt (採用；領養) 這三個字要一起背】

additional ﹝ ə'dɪʃənḷ ﹞ *adj.* 額外的

The waitress gave me an *additional* cup of coffee because I had to wait for my meal.【先背 add ﹝ æd ﹞ *v.* 加】

address ﹝ ə'drɛs , 'ædrɛs ﹞ *n.* 演說

He was invited to give the opening *address* at the ceremony.

【*give the opening address* 開幕致辭】

adept 〔 ə'dɛpt 〕 *adj.* 熟練的

An *adept* card player, Walt likes nothing better than a game of poker.

【adept = expert = skillful】

adhesive 〔 əd'hisɪv 〕 *adj.* 有黏性的

The *adhesive* tape wasn't strong enough, so the banner fell. 【*adhesive tape* 膠帶；它的動詞是 adhere (黏著)】

adjourn 〔 ə'dʒɝn 〕 *v.* 使暫停；休會

The judge *adjourned* the trial until the prosecutor could find the missing witness.

administrative 〔 əd'mɪnə,stretɪv 〕 *adj.* 行政的；管理的

Richard's performance in the job shows that he has great *administrative* ability.

【先背 administer 〔 əd'mɪnəstə 〕 *v.* 管理】

admission ﹙ əd'mɪʃən ﹚ *n.*
入場（許可）；入學（許可）

It is impossible to gain *admission* to
the club unless you are a VIP.

admit ﹙ əd'mɪt ﹚ *v.* 承認

I have to *admit* that I have made some
mistakes in dealing with the matter.

adoption ﹙ ə'dɑpʃən ﹚ *n.* 採用

The *adoption* of the
policy will cost much
money and time.

ad + opt + ion
│ │ │
to + 選擇 + *n.*

advance ﹙ əd'væns ﹚ *v.* 晉升；前進

A worker can *advance* to a better
position if he works hard.

adverse〔əd'vɝs〕*adj.* 不利的

We postponed the hike
because of the *adverse*
conditions.

```
ad + verse
 |     |
to + turn
```

【相反詞是 favorable〔'fevərəbḷ〕*adj.* 有利的】

advise〔əd'vaɪz〕*v.* 勸告

He *advised* his daughter not to marry in
a hurry.【名詞是 advice〔əd'vaɪs〕*n.* 勸告】

aerobic〔ˌeə'robɪk〕*adj.* 有氧的

Sharon does *aerobic* exercise for thirty
minutes every day to get slim.

【aero 是表 air（空氣）的字根；它的名詞是
aerobics（有氧運動）】

agenda〔ə'dʒɛndə〕*n.* 議程

The first item on the *agenda* is to
welcome the visitors.

agent ('edʒənt) *n.* 代理人

Mr. White is my *agent*;
he can make decisions
for me.

```
ag + ent
 |     |
act + 人
```

agreeable (ə'griəbḷ) *adj.* 心情愉快的

His employer appeared to be in such an
agreeable mood that Tom decided to ask
for a raise.

agreement (ə'grimənt) *n.* 協議；
同意

They reached an *agreement* only after
hours of discussion.

【*reach an agreement* 達成協議】

aim (em) *v.* 目標在於   *n.* 目標

The owner of the goods *aims* first at
protecting himself against losses.

air-conditioner ('ɛrkən'dɪʃənɚ) *n.*
冷氣機

Would someone please turn on the
air-conditioner? It's scorching in here!

airfare ('ɛr,fɛr) *n.* 飛機票價

How much is the *airfare* to France?

【airfare = air (空中) + fare (交通工具的票價)】

alert (ə'lɜt) *adj.* 機警的

The *alert* guard prevented a robbery.

allegedly (ə'lɛdʒɪdlɪ) *adv.* 據說

David was *allegedly* murdered by his
wife.

allocate ('ælə,ket) *v.* 分配

The charity *allocated*
the supplies to the
victims of the fire.

al	+	loc	+	ate
to	+	place	+	v.

alphabetical 〔͵ælfə'bɛtɪkl̩ 〕 *adj.*
字母的；按照字母順序的

The names in the address book are arranged in *alphabetical* order.

【alphabet 是指「整套字母」，即 A～Z，共 26 個字母，而 letter 則是指「一個字母」】

alter 〔'ɔltɚ 〕 *v.* 修改

I will need to have this suit *altered* before I can wear it. 【alter 表 other（別的）的字根】

alternate 〔'ɔltɚ͵net 〕 *v.* 輪流

We *alternate* the chore of taking out the garbage. 【alternate = *take turns at*】

alternative 〔 ɔl'tɜnətɪv 〕 *n.* 替代品

Scientists are looking for *alternatives* to replace some of the more expensive metals.

altitude 〔'æltə,tjud 〕 *n.* 高度

The hot-air balloon soon climbed to an *altitude* of 550 meters.

【不要與 latitude（緯度）搞混】

alt	+ itude
high	+ *n.*

ambassador 〔 æm'bæsədə 〕 *n.* 大使

Mr. Lee is our *ambassador* to South Africa.【embassy〔'ɛmbəsɪ〕是「大使館」】

amenity 〔 ə'mɛnətɪ 〕 *n.* 舒適

The *amenity* of the Hawaiian climate attracts a lot of vacationers.

analysis 〔 ə'næləsɪs 〕 *n.* 分析

His *analysis* of the data complete, Rob began to write his report.

【動詞是 analyze〔'ænḷ,aɪz〕 *v.* 分析】

announcement 〔 ə'naʊnsmənt 〕 n. 宣布

Our boss made an *announcement* that he will give us a raise in salary.

an + nounce + ment
| | |
to + *report* + *n.*

annoy 〔 ə'nɔɪ 〕 v. 使苦惱

He was greatly *annoyed* by the new and unexpected development.

【名詞是 annoyance (討厭的人或物)】

annual 〔 'ænjʊəl 〕 adj. 一年的；一年一度的

ann + ual
| |
year + *adj.*

That contract is effective for only one year; it is an *annual* one.

annum 〔 'ænəm 〕 n. 年

We hold a class reunion per *annum*.

anonymous 〔 ə'nɑnəməs 〕 adj. 匿名的

The *anonymous* letter was slipped under my door, so I have no idea where it came from.

an	+ onym	+ ous
|	|	|
without	+ *name*	+ *adj.*

antique 〔 æn'tik 〕 n. 古董

His grandfather's watch is a valuable *antique*.【注意字尾的 que 讀 / k /】

anxiety 〔 æŋ'zaɪətɪ 〕 n. 焦慮

The dentist tried to relieve his patient's *anxiety* by telling him his teeth were in good shape.【anxious 〔'æŋkʃəs〕 adj. 焦慮的】

appeal 〔 ə'pil 〕 v. 懇求

The students *appealed* for an extension on their homework assignment.

【此字也可與 to 連用，作「吸引」解】

appearance 〔ə'pɪrəns〕 n. 外表;出席

My father was not satisfied with my *appearance* and told me to get a haircut.

appetite 〔'æpə,taɪt〕 n. 食慾

James has no *appetite* for spicy food.

【飯前增進食慾的「開胃菜」叫作 appetizer】

applaud 〔ə'plɔd〕 v. 鼓掌

When the concert was over, the audience *applauded* enthusiastically.

【相反詞是 hiss〔hɪs〕v. 發出噓聲】

ap + plaud
  | |
to + clap

appliance 〔ə'plaɪəns〕 n. 家電用品

This washing machine was the first *appliance* we bought after we got married.

A

自我測驗

- ☐ abrupt _____
- ☐ access _____
- ☐ accordingly _____
- ☐ acknowledge _____
- ☐ acutely _____

- ☐ adhesive _____
- ☐ adoption _____
- ☐ agenda _____
- ☐ agent _____
- ☐ airfare _____

- ☐ alternative _____
- ☐ altitude _____
- ☐ annual _____
- ☐ anonymous _____
- ☐ appliance _____

✓ Check List ★

1.	缺　席	a _absence_ e	
2.	稱　讚	a ＿＿＿＿＿ m	
3.	會計師	a ＿＿＿＿＿ t	
4.	精確的	a ＿＿＿＿＿ e	
5.	額外的	a ＿＿＿＿＿ l	
6.	使暫停；休會	a ＿＿＿＿＿ n	
7.	晉升；前進	a ＿＿＿＿＿ e	
8.	不利的	a ＿＿＿＿＿ e	
9.	協議；同意	a ＿＿＿＿＿ t	
10.	分　配	a ＿＿＿＿＿ e	
11.	輪　流	a ＿＿＿＿＿ e	
12.	大　使	a ＿＿＿＿＿ r	
13.	宣　布	a ＿＿＿＿＿ t	
14.	焦　慮	a ＿＿＿＿＿ y	
15.	鼓　掌	a ＿＿＿＿＿ d	

applicable〔'æplɪkəbḷ〕*adj.* 適用的

Your example is not *applicable* to this case.【動詞是 apply（申請；應用）】

application〔͵æplə'keʃən〕*n.* 申請

Please fill out this *application* form before your interview.

appoint〔ə'pɔɪnt〕*v.* 指派；任命

Lisa was *appointed* marketing manager.

appraisal〔ə'prezḷ〕*n.* 鑑定

An *appraisal* of the house showed serious damage from the storm.

ap + prais + al
to + price + n.

appreciation〔ə͵priʃɪ'eʃən〕*n.* 感激；漲價

Mrs. Jones expressed her *appreciation* to the boy who found her lost dog.

apprehend ﹝͵æprɪˊhɛnd﹞ v. 逮捕

The shoplifter was *apprehended* when she tried to leave the store.

```
ap + prehend
 |      |
 to  +  seize
```

approach ﹝əˊprotʃ﹞ v. 接近　 n. 方法

Our dog always barks when strangers *approach* the house.

approve ﹝əˊpruv﹞ v. 贊成

To my surprise, my father *approved* of my plan to study abroad.

【相反詞是 disapprove﹝͵dɪsəˊpruv﹞ v. 不贊成】

approximately ﹝əˊprɑksəmɪtlɪ﹞ adv. 大約

The area of the vacant lot is *approximately* 300 square meters.

【approximately = about = around】

arrange 〔 ə'rendʒ 〕 *v.* 安排

The meeting has been *arranged* for tonight. 【arrange = schedule 】

array 〔 ə're 〕 *n.* 一長排

The waiter brought an *array* of fancy desserts to our table. 【先背 ray (光線)】

artificial 〔 ˌɑrtə'fɪʃəl 〕 *adj.* 人工的；人造的

This drink has few calories because it contains an *artificial* sweetener.

【*artificial sweetener* 人工甘味料 】

ascend 〔 ə'sɛnd 〕 *v.* 上升

The airplane *ascended* into the cloudy sky.

【相反詞是 descend (下降)】

```
a  +  scend
|       |
to  +  climb
```

assembly line　*n.* 裝配線

The problem with the *assembly line* caused a great loss to our company.

as + sembl + y
|　　|　　|
to + *same* + *n.*

assent 〔 ə'sɛnt 〕 *v. n.* 同意

All of us *assented* to Jason's proposal.

【assent (同意) 和 ascent (上升) 容易搞混】

assign 〔 ə'saɪn 〕 *v.* 指派

Our class leader *assigned* each of us a task.【assign = as + sign (簽名)】

assistance 〔 ə'sɪstəns 〕 *n.* 幫助

The government gave monetary *assistance* to the victims of the earthquake.

as + sist + ance
|　　|　　|
to + *stand* + *n.*

assume 〔ə'sum〕 v. 認爲

Never *assume* you have learned enough.
Knowledge is limitless.

【 assume = presume 】

as + sume
| |
to + *take*

asthma 〔'æzmə 〕 n. 氣喘

He can't participate in sports, because he
has a bad case of *asthma*. 【注意 th 不發音】

astonish 〔ə'stɑnɪʃ 〕 v. 使驚訝

We were *astonished* by the number of
the complaints. 【astonish = surprise 】

atmosphere 〔'ætməs,fɪr 〕 n.
大氣層；氣氛

The satellite will burn up when it
reenters the earth's
atmosphere.

atmo + sphere
| |
vapor + *ball*

attach 〔əˋtætʃ〕 v. 附加

I will *attach* the report to my next e-mail. 【*attach* A *to* B 把 A 附加在 B 上；名詞是 attachment（附件）】

attempt 〔əˋtɛmpt〕 v. n. 試圖

Jack and I will *attempt* to climb Mount Everest next year.

at	+	tempt
to	+	try

attendant 〔əˋtɛndənt〕 adj. 隨侍的

We hired an *attendant* nurse to take care of our ailing grandfather.

【attendant 也可當名詞用，作「服務員」解】

attorney 〔əˋtɝnɪ〕 n. 律師

It takes several years of study to become an *attorney*.

【attorney = lawyer】

at	+	torne	+	y
to	+	turn	+	n.

attraction 〔 əˈtrækʃən 〕 n.
吸引人的事物；觀光勝地

White beaches are one of the *attractions* of the island. 【tract 是表 draw (拉) 的字根】

attribute 〔 əˈtrɪbjut 〕 v. 歸因

I *attribute* my failure to a lack of preparation. 【attribute (歸因)、contribute (貢獻)，和 distribute (分配) 可一起背】

auction 〔ˈɔkʃən 〕 n. 拍賣

The house will be sold at *auction,* so the final price is not yet known.

auditor 〔ˈɔdɪtɚ 〕 n. 查帳員；旁聽生

The *auditor* found that the company's financial records had been kept inaccurately.

audit + or
  | |
hear + 人

auditorium 〔͵ɔdə'torɪəm 〕 *n.* 禮堂

The *auditorium* is the best place to hold the concert. 【-ium 是表「場所」的字尾】

authoritatively 〔 ə'θɔrə͵tetɪvlɪ 〕 *adv.* 命令式地

The boss *authoritatively* ordered all employees to work overtime for two days.

authorize 〔'ɔθə͵raɪz 〕 *v.* 授權

I have *authorized* my lawyers to act on my behalf. 【先背 author (作者)，賦予和作者相同的權利，即「授權」】

automated 〔'ɔtə͵metɪd 〕 *adj.* 自動化的

Our company has a fully *automated* factory.

auto +	mat	+ ed
self +	thinking +	adj.

available 〔 ə'veləbḷ 〕 *adj.* 可獲得的

The hotel is full. There are no rooms
available.

a + vail + able
| | |
to + worth + adj.

avenue 〔 'ævə,nju 〕 *n.* 大道；途徑

The restaurant is located
on First *Avenue*.

a + venue
| |
to + come

aware 〔 ə'wɛr 〕 *adj.* 知道的；察覺到的

He was *aware* of the danger.

【 *be aware of* 察覺到 (= *be conscious of*)；

　　它的相反詞是 unaware 】

awe 〔 ɔ 〕 *n.* 敬畏

Peter looked at his father in *awe*.

【形容詞是 awesome 〔 'ɔsəm 〕 *adj.* 令人敬畏的】

B b

banquet 〔'bæŋkwɪt〕 *n.* 宴會

A *banquet* will be held in honor of the
graduates.【*wedding banquet* 就是「喜宴」;
banquet = feast】

barely 〔'bɛrlɪ〕 *adv.* 幾乎不

Debbie is so tired that she can *barely* keep
her eyes open.【barely = scarcely = hardly】

bell captain   *n.* 男侍領班

Tom was promoted to *bell captain* last
month.【captain 是作「(旅館、飯店的)領班」
解,客人需要服務的時候,只要按 bell(鈴)】

benefit 〔'bɛnəfɪt〕 *n.* 福利;津貼

A personnel manager should give
information to employees about *benefits*,
vacations, and other jobs in the
company.【benefit 也作「利益;好處」解】

big-name (ˈbɪgˈnem) *adj.* 知名的

The *big-name* actor was involved in a scandal last year.

bilingualism (baɪˈlɪŋgwəlˌɪzəm) *n.*
能用兩種語言
Taiwan is trending
toward *bilingualism*.

bi + lingual + ism
| | |
two + 語言的 + *n.*

billing (ˈbɪlɪŋ) *n.* 廣告；宣傳

Because of the advance *billing*, the concert tickets were sold out one week before.【*advance billing* 事前的宣傳】

biochemistry (ˌbaɪoˈkɛmɪstrɪ) *n.*
生物化學
Biochemistry, seen as science's attempt to break the laws of nature, has always been a controversial topic.

【biochemistry = bio (*life*) + chemistry (化學)】

boast 〔 bost 〕 v. 自誇

It is not polite to *boast* of your successes.

【此字跟台語「自己褒才不會臭腥」
的「褒」發音很像】

bonus 〔'bonəs 〕 n. 贈品；獎金；紅利

If you buy four of this product, you will
receive one free as a *bonus*.

border 〔'bɔrdɚ 〕 n. 邊界

I live on the *border* between North Hills
and South Hills, so it is convenient for
me to go to either city. 【border = boundary 】

bound 〔 baʊnd 〕 adj. 被綑綁的

The police rescued the *bound* hostages,
but the thief managed to escape.

【bind (綁) 的過去式和過去分詞就是 bound 】

B

brake 〔 brek 〕 *n.* 煞車

The *brakes* on this car must be repaired before it is safe to drive.

【與 break（打破）的發音相同】

branch 〔 bræntʃ 〕 *n.* 樹枝；分店

There is a *branch* of Fidelity Bank on Main Street as well as one on Clark Avenue.

breach 〔 britʃ 〕 *n.* 違約

Our supplier did not deliver the goods by the date we agreed upon, so they are in *breach* of our contract.【breach = b + reach（達到），沒有達到要求，表示「違約」】

breakdown 〔'brek͵daʊn 〕 *n.* 故障

A busy highway wasn't a good place to have a *breakdown*.

【「故障」的片語就是 *break down*】

break-in ('brek,ın) *n.* 闖入

After a *break-in*, the storeowner installed a camera. 【「闖入」的片語就是 *break in*】

breathe (brið) *v.* 呼吸

To *breathe* fresh air in the forest is delightful. 【名詞為 breath (brεθ) *n.* 呼吸】

breed (brid) *v.* 生育;繁殖

The zookeepers tried in vain to *breed* the pandas.

brew (bru) *v.* 釀造

He *brews* his own beer at home.

【「釀造廠」是 brewery ('bruərı)】

brief (brif) *adj.* 簡短的

He gave a *brief* talk to the students.

【相反詞是 lengthy ('lεŋθı) *adj.* 冗長的】

brochure ﹝ bro'ʃur ﹞ *n.* 小冊子

The Wangs went to the travel agency
for some *brochures*.

【注意此字的發音；brochure = pamphlet】

broker ﹝'brokɚ﹞ *n.* 經紀人

A real estate *broker* helped us buy a new
house. 【*real estate broker* 房地產經紀人】

budget ﹝'bʌdʒɪt﹞ *n.* 預算

Paul was forced to cut his *budget* after
he lost his part-time job.

bulletin ﹝'bulətɪn﹞ *n.* 新聞快報；佈告

The weather bureau issued a *bulletin*
warning of an approaching typhoon.

【<u>bull</u>（公牛）-<u>bull</u>et（子彈）-<u>bull</u>etin（佈
告）要一起背】

- [ ] application   _____
- [ ] approve   _____
- [ ] ascend   _____
- [ ] assign   _____
- [ ] asthma   _____

- [ ] attempt   _____
- [ ] auction   _____
- [ ] auditorium   _____
- [ ] available   _____
- [ ] barely   _____

- [ ] billing   _____
- [ ] bonus   _____
- [ ] breakdown   _____
- [ ] brew   _____
- [ ] broker   _____

Check List

B

1. 指派；任命	a ___*appoint*___ t
2. 大 約	a _____ y
3. 安 排	a _____ e
4. 幫 助	a _____ e
5. 認 為	a _____ e
6. 附 加	a _____ h
7. 歸 因	a _____ e
8. 自動化的	a _____ d
9. 大道；途徑	a _____ e
10. 福利；津貼	b _____ t
11. 知名的	b _____ e
12. 自 誇	b _____ t
13. 違 約	b _____ h
14. 簡短的	b _____ f
15. 預 算	b _____ t

bureau (ˈbjʊro) *n.* 局

This map is published by the Tourist *Bureau*. 【*the Tourist Bureau* 觀光局；注意此字的字尾 eau 讀 / o / 】

C c

C.O.D. *n.* 貨到付款

(= *cash on delivery*)

We will send the goods *C.O.D.*; you can't pay on account.

cab (kæb) *n.* 計程車

Mary was late for the party, so she went by *cab*. 【cab = taxi 】

cabin (ˈkæbɪn) *n.* 小木屋；船艙；機艙

The hunter lived in a *cabin* in the woods.

C

calligraphy 〔 kə'lıgrəfı 〕 *n.* 書法

Calligraphy is an art form requiring
many years' study.

calli	+ graphy
|	|
beautiful +	*write*

candidate 〔'kændə,det 〕 *n.* 候選人

The voters found it difficult to choose
between the two *candidates*.

capacity 〔 kə'pæsətı 〕 *n.* 容量

The *capacity* of the hall is 500 people.

capitol 〔'kæpətl̩ 〕 *n.* 美國國會大廈；
州議會大廈

The *Capitol* rejected the treaty because it
would interfere with economic growth.

【與 capital（首都；資金）的發音相同】

C

captain ('kæptɪn) *n.* 隊長;船長

He is the *captain* of our
team.

```
capt + ain
 |      |
head +  人
```

carefree ('kɛr,fri) *adj.* 無憂無慮的

Until they begin school,
children are *carefree*.

```
care +  free
 |       |
擔心 + 免於…的
```

cargo ('kɑrgo) *n.* 貨物

The ship was carrying a *cargo* of steel.

【cargo = car + go,貨車出發是要運送貨物】

carrier ('kærɪɚ) *n.* 運送人;郵差

The *carrier* delivers mail to our house
by 3:00. 【carrier = *mail carrier*】

carve (kɑrv) *v.* 雕刻

He *carved* the wood into the
shape of a bird. 【carve = sculpture】

case law *n.* 判例法

Mr. Brown teaches *case law* at the college.【case 是作「判例」解】

catalog (ˈkætḷˌɔg) *n.* 目錄

If something is not available in our store, you can order it from the *catalog*.

```
cata +  log
  |      |
fully + speak (詳細敘述的東西)
```

cater (ˈketɚ) *v.* 提供酒菜

Our company will *cater* delicious desserts for the party.

cellular phone *n.* 行動電話

Today *cellular phones* play an important role in our lives.

【*cellular phone* = *cell phone* = *mobile phone*】

C

certificate〔sə'tɪfəkɪt〕 *n.* 證書

She holds a *certificate* that says she worked here as a typist from 1960 to 1968.【先背 certify〔'sɝtə,faɪ〕*v.* 證明】

chain〔tʃen〕 *n.* 鍊子

My neighbor ties up his dog with a *chain* so that it won't run away.

【*chain store* 則是「連鎖店」】

chairman〔'tʃɛrmən〕 *n.* 主席

He was *chairman* of the meeting.

【「女主席」是 chairwoman；因爲女權意識 抬頭，爲了避免有性別歧視之虞，則會用 chairperson 這個中性的字】

character〔'kærɪktɚ〕 *n.* 個性

She has a changeable *character*.

【character = personality】

charge 〔tʃɑrdʒ〕 v. 收費;控告

The video store *charges* one hundred dollars for each DVD you borrow.

【此字也可當名詞用,作「責任」解,如 *in charge of* (負責)】

charitable 〔'tʃærətəbḷ〕 adj. 慈善的

Giving money to that beggar was a *charitable* act.

charity drive n. 慈善活動

The company organized a *charity drive* to establish a good image.

chart 〔tʃɑrt〕 n. 圖表

The result is shown on *chart* 2.

charter 〔'tʃɑrtɚ〕 v. 租 (交通工具)

We had to *charter* a private airplane.

【此字也可作「給予…執照;許可」解】

C

chastise〔tʃæsˈtaɪz〕v. 嚴厲地譴責

People who are cruel to animals should be *chastised*.

checkup〔ˈtʃɛkˌʌp〕n. 健康檢查

It is time for your *checkup* with the doctor.【checkup = *physical examination*】

chemical〔ˈkɛmɪkḷ〕adj. 化學的

Joe has decided to be a *chemical* engineer.【此字也可當名詞用，作「化學藥品」解】

chew〔tʃu〕v. 嚼

Please don't *chew* gum in class.

chore〔tʃor〕n. 雜事

George and Mary shared the household *chores* between them.

【*household chores* 家事】

circulation (ˌsɝkjəˈleʃən) *n.* 循環

My sister often feels cold because she has poor *circulation*.

【 *have poor circulation* （血液的）循環不好 】

```
circul + at(e) + ion
  |        |       |
circle  +  v.  +  n. ( 繞著圈圈運轉 )
```

civic (ˈsɪvɪk) *adj.* 市民的

To vote is a *civic* duty of people in a democracy.【「市民」是 citizen (ˈsɪtəzn̩)】

clearance (ˈklɪrəns) *n.* 出入港許可證

You can't get your luggage without *clearance* from customs.【此字也可作「清掃」解，*clearance sale* 則是「清倉大拍賣」】

client (ˈklaɪənt) *n.* 客戶

The salesman had an important meeting with his *client*.

climate (ˈklaɪmɪt) *n.* 氣候

The *climate* here is very hot and humid.

C

clutter (ˈklʌtɚ) *n.* 亂成一團；雜亂

Sophia got angry when she saw her room
was in a *clutter*. 【*in a clutter* 雜亂的】

coherent (koˈhɪrənt) *adj.* 有條理的；
前後一致的

This plan is *coherent*; all of the parts
work well together.

co	+ her	+ ent
together	+ stick	+ adj.

colleague (ˈkɑlig) *n.* 同事

Professor Lee is a *colleague*
of Professor Pan.

【colleague = co-worker】

col	+ league
together	+ bind

C

comeback ('kʌm,bæk) *n.* 東山再起

Although his business failed, Mr. Smith didn't give up but made a *comeback*.

comment ('kamɛnt) *n.* 評論

He made no *comment* on the recent topics. 【不要與 commend（稱讚）搞混】

com	+ ment
|	|
thoroughly	+ *mind*

commerce ('kamɝs) *n.* 商業

Commerce is often said to be the exchange and distribution of goods on a large scale. 【形容詞是 commercial（商業的）】

commission (kə'mıʃən) *n.* 佣金

The real estate agent's *commission* is 15% of the selling price.

【commission = com + mission（任務）】

C

commit〔kəˈmɪt〕v. 委託；犯（罪）

It is hoped that fear of punishment will
prevent people from *committing* crimes.
【*commit a crime* 犯罪】

committee〔kəˈmɪtɪ〕n. 委員會

The planning *committee* is made up of
15 members.【-ee 是表「被～的人」的字尾】

commodity〔kəˈmadətɪ〕n. 商品

Investors buy large amounts of
commodities and hope that the price
increases.

com	+ mod + ity
|	|　　|
together	*+ kind + n.*

commune〔ˈkamjun〕n. 公社

There is no private property in this
commune, and food is distributed equally.
【commune 是表 common（共同的）的字根，
如 communism〔ˈkamjuˌnɪzəm〕n. 共產主義】

commute〔kə'mjut〕v. 通勤

Not all of the students live on campus.
Those who live near the university can
commute by bus.

com	+	mute
together	+	change

compatible〔kəm'pætəbḷ〕adj.
合得來的；相容的

He and his wife were not *compatible*
and they decided to divorce.

com	+	pat	+	ible
together	+	suffer	+	adj.

compensation〔͵kɑmpən'seʃən〕n.
賠償

Mark paid NT$100,000 in *compensation*
for the car accident.

C

competitive ﹝ kəm'pɛtətɪv ﹞ *adj.*
競爭激烈的

We will have a *competitive* examination next Monday. 【compete ﹝ kəm'pit ﹞ *v.* 競爭】

complacency ﹝ kəm'plesn̩sɪ ﹞ *n.*
得意；自滿

Too much *complacency* caused the defeat.

com	+ plac	+ ency
|	|	|
thoroughly	+ *please* +	*n.*

complaint ﹝ kəm'plent ﹞ *n.* 抱怨

The students are full of *complaints* about the food in the cafeteria.

component ﹝ kəm'ponənt ﹞ *n.* 成分；
構成要素

Volunteer workers are one *component* of our plan to make money from the fair.

compose 〔 kəm'poz 〕 v. 組成；作 (曲)

The band is *composed* of both boys and girls. 【 *be composed of* 由~組成 】

com	+ pose
together	+ *put*

compost 〔'kɑmpost 〕 n. 堆肥

Karen mixes *compost* and soil to plant flowers.

comprehension 〔 ˌkɑmprɪ'hɛnʃən 〕 n. 理解

He always acts as if he understands in Japanese class, but his *comprehension* is not that good, actually.

【 *reading comprehension test* 就是「閱讀 測驗」】

com	+ prehens	+ ion
completely	+ *seize*	+ *n.*

comprise 〔 kəm'praɪz 〕 v. 組成；包含

The national team will be *comprised* of the best players from all the high schools in Taiwan.

【 *be comprised of* = comprise = *be composed of* = *be made up of* 】

concept 〔'kɑnsɛpt 〕 n. 觀念

It is difficult for young children to understand abstract *concepts*.

conclude 〔 kən'klud 〕 v. 下結論

The jury *concluded* that she was not guilty.

【名詞是 conclusion (結論)】

```
con + clude
 |      |
all + close
```

conduct 〔 kən'dʌkt 〕 v. 進行；做

We will have to *conduct* many experiments in our science class.

自我測驗

C

- [ ] C.O.D. _____
- [ ] capacity _____
- [ ] carrier _____
- [ ] cater _____
- [ ] certificate _____

- [ ] charge _____
- [ ] chore _____
- [ ] clearance _____
- [ ] clutter _____
- [ ] comment _____

- [ ] commodity _____
- [ ] compensation _____
- [ ] component _____
- [ ] comprehension _____
- [ ] conclude _____

Check List

C

1. 局　　　　　　b _bureau_ u

2. 候選人　　　　c _____ e

3. 貨　物　　　　c _____ o

4. 目　錄　　　　c _____ g

5. 主　席　　　　c _____ n

6. 慈善的　　　　c _____ e

7. 健康檢查　　　c _____ p

8. 客　戶　　　　c _____ t

9. 同　事　　　　c _____ e

10. 佣　金　　　　c _____ n

11. 委員會　　　　c _____ e

12. 通　勤　　　　c _____ e

13. 競爭激烈的　　c _____ e

14. 觀　念　　　　c _____ t

15. 進行；做　　　c _____ t

confer〔kən'fɝ〕*v.* 商議

The President often *confers* with his advisers on diplomatic problems.

【它的名詞是 conference（會議）】

confide〔kən'faɪd〕*v.* （因信賴而）透露

Carol *confided* to me that she likes Mike.

【confident（有信心的）和 confidential（機密的）這兩 個形容詞的意思不要搞混】

con + fide	
|	|
fully +	*trust*

confirmation〔ˌkɑnfɚ'meʃən〕*n.* 確認；證實

There has been no *confirmation* of the news about the financial crisis of the company.【先背 firm（堅固的）】

confiscate〔'kɑnfɪsˌket〕*v.* 沒收

The customs official *confiscated* the apples because travelers are not allowed to bring fresh food into the country.

C

conflict ('kɑnflɪkt) *n.* 衝突

They have a *conflict* in what they believe.

con	+	flict
|		|
together	+	*strike*

conscience ('kɑnʃəns) *n.* 良心

My *conscience* bothered me after I told a lie. 【conscience = con + science (科學)；它的形容詞是 conscientious (有良心的)，唸作 (ˌkɑnʃɪ'ɛnʃəs)】

conscious ('kɑnʃəs) *adj.* 有意識的

The man was knocked out in the accident, but he is *conscious* now.

consecutive (kən'sɛkjətɪv) *adj.*
連續的 (= *successive*)

Our team won, finally, after three *consecutive* losses.

【secut 和 sequ 都是表 follow (跟隨) 的字根】

C

consensus ﹝kən'sɛnsəs﹞ *n.* 共識

After much discussion we reached a *consensus*.【先背 sense (感覺)】

consent ﹝kən'sɛnt﹞ *v.* 同意

I asked my parents to let me go out this Friday, but they did not *consent*.

【consent = assent = agree】

consequently ﹝'kɑnsə,kwɛntlɪ﹞ *adv.* 因此

She ate too much cake and *consequently* was sick.【形容詞是 consequent (接著發生的)，名詞是 consequence (結果)】

conserve ﹝kən'sɝv﹞ *v.* 節省；保護

We must *conserve* natural resources so that our children may have a better world to live in.

con + serve
| |
all + *keep*

C

consideration ﹝ kənˌsɪdəˈreʃən ﹞ *n.*
考慮
We should take several things into
consideration before we decide
something important.
【*take…into consideration* 考慮到…】

consistent ﹝ kənˈsɪstənt ﹞ *adj.* 一致的
Your stories are not *consistent*, so one of
you must be lying. 【相反詞是 contradictory
﹝ˌkɑntrəˈdɪktərɪ﹞ *adj.* 矛盾的】

consolidate ﹝ kənˈsɑləˌdet ﹞ *v.*
合併（支出）
Friends who share an apartment may
consolidate expenses.

con	+ solid +	ate
wholly +	固體 +	*v.*

constant (ˈkɑnstənt) *adj.* 不斷的

There has been a *constant* rain since Friday. 【constant = continual】

constrain (kənˈstren) *v.* 限制

Marriage usually will *constrain* the closeness of the couple's new friendships.

con	+ strain
together +	拉緊

constraint

(kənˈstrent) *n.* 強迫;束縛

Emily is tired of the *constraints* of high school and cannot wait to experience a freer life.

construction (kənˈstrʌkʃən) *n.* 建造

The latest technology was used in the *construction* of this building.

【struct 是表 build (建造) 的字根】

consult〔kən'sʌlt〕*v.* 請教；查閱

If you feel ill, you should *consult* a doctor.【名詞是 consultant（顧問）】

containment〔kən'tenmənt〕*n.* 圍堵；抑制

America decided to follow an economic *containment* policy with North Korea in punishment for its development of nuclear weapons.【先背 contain（包含）】

contaminated〔kən'tæmə,netɪd〕*adj.* 受到污染的（= *polluted*）

Many people were hospitalized after drinking *contaminated* water.

contemplate〔'kɑntəm,plet〕*v.* 仔細考慮

Vicky *contemplated* whether to take the job or not.【contemplate = con (*wholly*) + templ(e)（寺廟）+ ate (*v.*)】

content 〔'kɑntɛnt〕 *n.* 內容
〔kən'tɛnt〕 *adj.* 滿足的

The detective asked me to show him the *contents* of my pockets.

continent 〔'kɑntənənt〕 *n.* 洲；大陸

The explorer has traveled to all seven *continents*.

contract 〔'kɑntrækt〕 *n.* 合約
〔kən'trækt〕 *v.* 收縮；感染

We have a *contract* with that company.

contradict 〔,kɑntrə'dɪkt〕 *v.*
反駁；與…矛盾

Henry's father hit the ceiling because Henry *contradicted* him.

contra + dict
| |
against + say

contribution 〔͵kɑntrə'bjuʃən 〕 *n.*
捐贈；貢獻

The millionaire made a large
contribution to the orphanage.

【 *make a contribution to⋯* 向⋯捐獻 】

con	+ tribut(e) + ion
|	| |
together +	貢物 + *n.*

convention 〔 kən'vɛnʃən 〕 *n.* 定期會議

The doctors' *convention* was held in
Kaohsiung.【形容詞是 conventional（傳
統的)】

con	+ vent + ion
|	| |
together +	*come* + *n.*

convince 〔 kən'vɪns 〕 *v.* 說服

Danny *convinced* his parents to get a dog
by promising to take care of it.

【 *convince sb. to V.* 說服某人做某事 】

cooperative 〔 ko'ɑpə,retɪv 〕 *adj.*
合作的

All of the farmers have a stake in the *cooperative* store where they sell their produce.

co	+ operat(e)	+ ive
together +	操作	+ *adj.*

coordinator 〔 ko'ɔrdə,netɚ 〕 *n.* 協調人

Emily was chosen to be the *coordinator* of the program; she will direct all of our efforts.

co	+ ordin	+ at(e)	+ or
with +	order +	*v.*	+ 人

cordially 〔'kɔrdʒəlɪ 〕 *adv.* 熱忱地

The host and hostess *cordially* welcomed their foreign guests.

cord	+ ial	+ ly
heart	+ *adj.*	+ *adv.*

corporation (͵kɔrpəˈreʃən) *n.* 公司

The *corporation* has expanded its business overseas.

【corporation = company = firm = enterprise】

correspondingly (͵kɔrəˈspandɪŋlɪ)
adv. 對應地

The senior members have more rights and, *correspondingly*, more responsibilities. 【先背 respond (反應)】

corruption (kəˈrʌpʃən) *n.* 貪污

When it was found that another official had been taking bribes, the president vowed to wipe out *corruption* in his government once and for all.

cor	+ rupt	+ ion
all	+ break	+ n.

costly ('kɔstlɪ) *adj.* 昂貴的

Buying the wrong software was a *costly* mistake. 【costly = expensive 】

counterpart ('kauntɚ,part) *n.* 相對應的人或事物

The American President's *counterpart* in England is their Prime Minister.

```
counter + part
  |         |
against + part
```

coupon ('kupan) *n.* 優待券

This *coupon* entitles you to a free drink with your meal.

courier ('kurɪɚ , 'kɝɪɚ) *n.* 急件的遞送人

A bicycle *courier* in New York earns a lot of money. 【跟 carrier (郵差) 只差兩個字母】

C

courteously 〔'kɜtɪəslɪ 〕 *adv.* 有禮貌地

All of the waiters in the hotel serve customers *courteously*.【相反詞是 rudely（無禮地）; 名詞是 courtesy〔'kɜtəsɪ 〕 *n.* 禮貌】

cover letter *n.* 附信

Other related information about this plan is in the *cover letter*.

coverage 〔'kʌvərɪdʒ 〕 *n.* 報導

Local media organizations rely on foreign news agencies for world news *coverage*.【coverage = cover（涵蓋）+ age (*n.*)，報導內容會涵蓋多方面的消息】

creative 〔 krɪ'etɪv 〕 *adj.* 有創造力的

Tom is a very *creative* boy; he always has neat ideas.

cre	+ at(e)	+ ive
|	|	|
make	+ *v.*	+ *adj.*

crew〔kru〕*n.* 一群工作人員

The ship carries a *crew* of thirty men.

【當此字是指一個整體時，動詞要用單數；指個別成員時，動詞則用複數。crew = staff】

cruise〔kruz〕*n.* 巡航；周遊

At Sun Moon Lake, you can take a *cruise* for a few hundred dollars.

【*take a cruise* （坐遊艇、汽船等）巡航；cruise 源自於 cross（越過；交叉；十字）】

crystal〔'krɪstḷ〕*n.* 水晶

The river was as clear as *crystal* before, but now it has been polluted.

【*as clear as crystal* 清澈的】

culminate〔'kʌlmə,net〕*v.* 終於成為

We hoped the search would *culminate* in a new discovery.

【此字為不及物動詞，介系詞要用 in】

currency (ˈkɝənsɪ) *n.* 貨幣

Devaluation is an official
decrease in the par value
of a nation's *currency*.

curr + ency
| |
run + *n.*

【「外幣」則是 *foreign currency*】

currently (ˈkɝəntlɪ) *adv.* 目前；現在

Sarah is *currently* an assistant, but she
will be promoted to manager soon due to
her effort.【currently = presently】

curriculum (kəˈrɪkjələm) *n.* 課程

Our school *curriculum* features cooking
classes for boys.【形容詞是 curricular（課
程的），extracurricular 則是指「課外的」】

custom (ˈkʌstəm) *n.* 習俗

It's a *custom* for Japanese to bow when
they meet their acquaintances.

customs (ˈkʌstəmz) *n.* 海關

The man was stopped at *customs* for carrying drugs.

D d

deadlock (ˈdɛdˌlɑk) *n.* 僵局

Labor and management have been unable to break the *deadlock* in their negotiations.
【deadlock = dead (死的) + lock (鎖)】

deal (dil) *n.* 交易   *v.* 處理 < *with* >

We have made a *deal* with a big auto company to supply all of their spare parts.
【口語常説的 It's a deal. 表示「一言爲定。」】

decade (ˈdɛked) *n.* 十年

Over the last *decade*, writer-director David Mamet has made many great films.

dec(a) + ade
| |
ten + *n.*

- [ ] confer _____
- [ ] conflict _____
- [ ] consensus _____
- [ ] consolidate _____
- [ ] constant _____

- [ ] contemplate _____
- [ ] contract _____
- [ ] convention _____
- [ ] coordinator _____
- [ ] corruption _____

- [ ] counterpart _____
- [ ] creative _____
- [ ] cruise _____
- [ ] currency _____
- [ ] customs _____

D

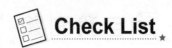

1. 確認；證實   c _confirmation_ n
2. 有意識的   c _____ s
3. 節省；保護   c _____ e
4. 一致的   c _____ t
5. 限　制   c _____ n

6. 受到污染的   c _____ d
7. 內容；滿足的   c _____ t
8. 捐贈；貢獻   c _____ n
9. 合作的   c _____ e
10. 公　司   c _____ n

11. 優待券   c _____ n
12. 報　導   c _____ e
13. 一群工作人員   c _____ w
14. 目前；現在   c _____ y
15. 交易；處理   d _____ l

decision〔 dɪˈsɪʒən 〕 *n.* 決定

They made their *decision* after making
careful calculations.

【 *make a decision* 做決定 】

de + cis + ion
| | |
off + *cut* + *n.*

D

deck〔 dɛk 〕 *n.* 甲板

They placed the cargo on the *deck* of the
ship.【 d<u>e</u>ck (甲板) 和 d<u>o</u>ck (碼頭) 不要搞混 】

decline〔 dɪˈklaɪn 〕 *v.* 下降;衰退;拒絕

Despite the new advertising campaign,
sales for this quarter actually *declined*.

de + cline
| |
down + *bend* (彎曲)

decorate〔 ˈdɛkəˌret 〕 *v.* 裝飾

The hotel room was *decorated* with
flowers.【 名詞是 decoration (裝飾;裝潢)】

defect (ˈdifɛkt , dɪˈfɛkt) *n.* 瑕疵;缺點

I was able to buy the stereo at a low price because it has a slight *defect*.

【相反詞是 perfection (完美)】

deficiently (dɪˈfɪʃəntlɪ) *adv.* 不足地

Doris didn't pass the exam because she was *deficiently* prepared for it.

de	+ fici	+ ent	+ ly
|	|	|	|
down	+ *do*	+ *adj.*	+ *adv.*

deficit (ˈdɛfəsɪt) *n.* 赤字【注意發音】

With the expenditure of $100,000 and an income of $60,000, the *deficit* is $40,000.

delegate (ˈdɛləˌget) *v.* 指派⋯為代表
n. 代表

He was *delegated* to the convention.

【先背 gate (大門),代表一個公司的門面】

deliberately (dɪˈlɪbərɪtlɪ) *adv.* 故意地

Mary *deliberately* came home late to avoid meeting her cousin.

【 deliberately = intentionally = *on purpose* 】

delicate (ˈdɛləkət , -kɪt) *adj.* 精緻的

Grandmother has a large collection of *delicate* porcelain.

【不要跟 dedicate (奉獻；使致力於) 搞混 】

delight (dɪˈlaɪt) *v.* 使高興

Circuses never fail to *delight* children.

【 delight = de + light (光線)】

delinquent (dɪˈlɪŋkwənt) *adj.* 拖欠的；犯法的

Try not to become *delinquent* in payment of your taxes. 【名詞是 delinquency (罪行)，*juvenile delinquency* 是指「青少年犯罪」】

deliver 〔 dɪˈlɪvɚ 〕 v. 遞送；發表（演說）
The postman *delivers* letters to our home every day.

demolish 〔 dɪˈmɑlɪʃ 〕 v. 拆除
The government has declined to *demolish* the whole building.
【demolish = *tear down* = *pull down*】

dense 〔 dɛns 〕 adj. 濃密的；密集的
There was little light in the *dense* forest.
【相反詞是 sparse（稀疏的；稀少的）】

depart 〔 dɪˈpɑrt 〕 v. 出發
Buses *depart* for the airport every twenty minutes.【相反詞是 arrive（抵達）】

deport 〔 dɪˈport 〕 v. 驅逐出境
Byron got *deported* because his visa had expired.【deport = de (*away*) + port（港口）】

deposit ﹝ dɪˈpɑzɪt ﹞ v. 存（錢）

n. 存款；定金

People *deposit* their money in the bank to keep it safe.

【相反詞是 withdraw「提（款）」】

description ﹝ dɪˈskrɪpʃən ﹞ n. 描述

Ann and David gave us a vivid *description* of their trip.

【動詞是 describe ﹝ dɪˈskraɪb ﹞】

designate ﹝ˈdɛzɪɡˌnet ﹞ v. 命名

The southern territory was *designated* Louisiana after the French monarch King Louis XVI.

de	+ sign	+ ate
down	+ *mark*	+ *v.*

desirable ﹝ dɪˈzaɪrəbḷ ﹞ adj. 理想的

Mr. and Mrs. Smith decided to buy the house for the *desirable* surroundings.

D

despair〔dɪ'spɛr〕n. 絕望

In his *despair*, Ken could
see no way to continue.

de + spair
| |
away + hope

【*in* one's *despair* 在絕望中】

destination〔ˌdɛstə'neʃən〕n. 目的地

Do you know what time we will reach
our *destination*?

【*reach* one's *destination* 抵達目的地】

detach〔dɪ'tætʃ〕v. 使分離;脫離

Some of them *detached*
themselves from the
party.

de + tach
| |
away + stake

detection〔dɪ'tɛkʃən〕n. 發現

Without the dogs' keen sense of smell,
detection of the gas leak would have
been impossible.【動詞是 detect】

deteriorate (dɪ'tɪrɪə‚ret) *v.* 惡化

If you don't take care of the garden, it will *deteriorate* and turn into a jungle.

【deteriorate = worsen】

D

determine (dɪ'tɜmɪn) *v.* 決定

The judge will *determine* which side is at fault.

de	+ termine
down +	limit

device (dɪ'vaɪs) *n.* 裝置

A microwave is a handy *device* for heating up food quickly.

【動詞是 devise (dɪ'vaɪz) *v.* 設計；想出】

diabetic (‚daɪə'bɛtɪk) *n.* 糖尿病患者

Diabetics are likely to suffer cardiovascular diseases.

【diabetes (‚daɪə'bitɪs , -tiz) *n.* 糖尿病】

diagnose (ˌdaɪəg'nos) v. 診斷

The doctor said he would need to run some tests before he could *diagnose* my illness.

【名詞是 diagnosis】

dia	+ gnose
apart	+ know

dimension (də'mɛnʃən) n. 尺寸；次元；…度空間

The *dimensions* of the mansion are enormous.

di	+ mension
apart	+ measure

director (də'rɛktɚ) n. 導演；主任

The *director* asked the actors to repeat their lines.【動詞是 direct (指導)】

directory (də'rɛktərɪ) n. 電話簿

You'll find his number in the telephone *directory*.

disabled 〔 dɪs'eblḍ 〕 *adj.* 殘障的

This is a special school for the physically *disabled*.【disabled = handicapped】

D

discard 〔 dɪs'kard 〕 *v.* 丟棄

Nancy peeled eight apples for the pie and *discarded* the peels.

dis	+	card
away	+	卡片

disclose 〔 dɪs'kloz 〕 *v.* 透露

The judge threatened the journalist with jail if he did not *disclose* the name of his source.

【相反詞是 conceal (隱瞞)】

dis	+	close
not	+	*shut*

discount 〔'dɪskaʊnt 〕 *n.* 折扣

To celebrate its 20th anniversary, this department store is selling everything at a *discount*.【先背 count (計算)，不列入計算】

disengaged 〔͵dɪsɪn'gedʒd〕*adj.* 空閒的

Since we will be *disengaged* this
Saturday, let's go to the movies.

【先背 engage（從事；忙於）】

dismal 〔'dɪzml̩〕*adj.* 陰暗的

The weather has been
dismal for days because it
has not stopped raining.

dis + mal
| |
days + bad

dismiss 〔dɪs'mɪs〕*v.* 解散；解僱

The workers were *dismissed* temporarily
from work.

dis + miss
| |
away + send

dismount 〔dɪs'maʊnt〕*v.* 從⋯下來

Alan *dismounted* from his motorcycle
and fastened a lock on it.

【先背 mount（登上；爬上；騎乘）】

D

dispatch (dɪ'spætʃ) v. 派遣

They *dispatched* a soldier to inform the general of the emergency.

【dispatch = *send out*】

dispenser (dɪ'spɛnsɚ) n.
藥劑師；自動販賣機

Sara bought a can of orange juice from the soft-drink *dispenser*.

dis	+ pens	+ er
out	pay	n.

disperse (dɪ'spɝs) v. 散開

The crowd *dispersed* when the police threatened to use tear gas.

di	+ sperse
apart	scatter

displace (dɪs'ples) v. 取代；
強迫（某人）離開

War is sure to *displace* much of the population. 【位置被拿掉，就表示要離開】

disposal 〔 dɪ'spozḷ 〕 *n.* 處理

People generate a lot of trash and its
disposal is becoming a problem.

【形容詞是 disposable（用完即丟的）】

dispute 〔 dɪ'spjut 〕 *v.* 爭論

The sisters *disputed* which of their
favorite singers was really the best.

【 dispute = argue 】

disrupt 〔 dɪs'rʌpt 〕 *v.* 使中斷

The protesters chanted
loudly outside, trying to
disrupt the meeting.

dis	+	rupt
|		|
apart	+	*break*

dissolve 〔 dɪ'zɑlv 〕 *v.* 溶解

Sugar will *dissolve*
quickly in a hot drink.

dis	+	solve
|		|
apart	+	解決

distinct ﹝ dɪ'stɪŋkt ﹞ *adj.* 明顯的

There is a *distinct* difference between the two wines and that is why one is much more expensive.

distinguish ﹝ dɪ'stɪŋgwɪʃ ﹞ *v.* 辨別

The twins were so much alike that it was impossible to *distinguish* one from the other. 【*distinguish* A *from* B 辨別 A 和 B】

distract ﹝ dɪ'strækt ﹞ *v.* 使分心

The driver was *distracted* by a dog running across the road and had an accident as a result.

dis	+ tract
apart	+ draw

distribute ﹝ dɪ'strɪbjʊt ﹞ *v.* 分配

We will *distribute* the new product to as many drugstores as possible.

district ('dɪstrɪkt) *n.* 地區

The waterfall is the most outstanding feature of this *district*.

di	+	strict
apart +	*draw tight*	

dividend ('dɪvə,dɛnd) *n.* 股利

The company is issuing *dividends* to its shareholders. 【先背 divide (də'vaɪd) *v.* 劃分;「股票」則是 stock】

division (də'vɪʒən) *n.* 劃分;分配

Betty complained about her brother's *division* of the cake, saying that he had taken the larger piece.

divorce (də'vors) *v.* 離婚

When a couple marries, neither expects to *divorce* later on.

di	+ vorce
apart +	*turn*

dock 〔 dɑk 〕 *n.* 碼頭

The passengers waved good-bye to the islanders as their ship moved away from the *dock*.

doctorate 〔'dɑktərɪt 〕 *n.* 博士學位

Jenny obtained a *doctorate* in economics.

【 *obtain a doctorate* 獲得博士學位；

「碩士」叫作 master 〔'mæstɚ 〕，

「學士」則是 bachelor 〔'bætʃələ 〕】

document 〔'dɑkjəmənt 〕 *n.* 文件

A birth certificate is an important *document*.【形容詞是 documentary (文書的)，但它也可當名詞用，作「記錄片」解 】

downsize 〔'daʊn'saɪz 〕 *v.* 裁減人數

When IBM *downsized* in 1995, it laid off employees.【相反詞是 expand (擴大)】

自我測驗

D

- [ ] decline _____
- [ ] defect _____
- [ ] deliberately _____
- [ ] deliver _____
- [ ] description _____

- [ ] destination _____
- [ ] deteriorate _____
- [ ] diagnose _____
- [ ] discount _____
- [ ] dismiss _____

- [ ] displace _____
- [ ] dissolve _____
- [ ] distribute _____
- [ ] dividend _____
- [ ] downsize _____

Check List

1. 甲　板　　　d ___deck___ k
2. 赤　字　　　d _____ t
3. 精緻的　　　d _____ e
4. 出　發　　　d _____ t
5. 存（錢）　　d _____ t

6. 發　現　　　d _____ n
7. 裝　置　　　d _____ e
8. 導演；主任　d _____ r
9. 透　露　　　d _____ e
10. 空閒的　　　d _____ d

11. 派　遣　　　d _____ h
12. 使中斷　　　d _____ t
13. 辨　別　　　d _____ h
14. 地　區　　　d _____ t
15. 文　件　　　d _____ t

D

downturn ('daʊn,tɜn) *n.* 下降

The *downturn* in the economy made unemployment rise.【upturn 則是「上升」】

drape (drep) *v.* 覆蓋

You may *drape* a scarf over the lampshade to dim the light.

drawback ('drɔ,bæk) *n.* 缺點

Many pure metals are too soft, rust too easily, or have some other *drawbacks*.

【drawback = draw (拉) + back (往後)】

due (dju) *adj.* 到期的

The gas bill is *due*, so you had better pay it right away.【overdue 則是「過期的」】

duplicate ('djupləkɪt) *n.* 副本

Would you mind making a *duplicate* of this for me?

【duplicate = copy 】

du	+ plic	+ ate
two	+ fold	+ n.

durability (ˌdjʊrəˈbɪlətɪ) *n.* 耐久性

The *durability* of the equipment is such that it will last for 10 years.

dur + ab(le) + ility
| | |
last + *adj.* + *n.*

duty (ˈdjutɪ) *n.* 責任；關稅

The *duty* of a student is to study.

【duty-free 是指「免稅的」】

E e

eager (ˈigɚ) *adj.* 渴望的；急切的

The birthday boy was so *eager* to open his present that he even forgot to say thank you.

earnest (ˈɝnɪst) *adj.* 眞誠的

Tim appreciated his brother's *earnest* desire to help him. 【earnest = sincere】

earnings 〔'ɜnɪŋz 〕 *n. pl.* 收入

Mary is very happy because this year her *earnings* increased a lot.【動詞是 earn（賺）】

echo 〔'ɛko 〕 *n.* 回音

The *echo* of our shouts gradually diminished.

E

ecology 〔 ɪ'kɑlədʒɪ 〕 *n.* 生態學

Joyce is studying *ecology* at university.

eco + logy
| |
house + study

economical 〔 ͵ikə'nɑmɪkl̩ 〕 *adj.* 節省的

Economical shoppers wait for special sales.【不要跟 economic（經濟的）搞混】

eco-tour 〔'iko͵tʊr 〕 *n.* 生態旅遊

Sam and his family are going on an *eco-tour* of Taroko National Park next month.

edge〔 ɛdʒ 〕 *n.* 邊緣

My mother is sitting on the *edge* of my younger brother's bed.

effective〔 ɪˈfɛktɪv 〕 *adj.* 有效的

The government should take some *effective* measures to solve the problem.

【名詞是 effect (影響)】

ef	+ fect	+ ive
|	|	|
out	+ do	+ adj.

efficiently〔 əˈfɪʃəntlɪ 〕 *adv.* 有效率地

The newly imported machine can manufacture goods *efficiently*.

elaborate〔 ɪˈlæbəˌret 〕 *v.* 詳述
〔 ɪˈlæbərɪt 〕 *adj.* 精巧的

Could you please *elaborate* on your ideas about this issue?

e	+ labor	+ ate
|	|	|
out	+ work	+ v.

electorate ﹝ ɪ'lɛktərɪt ﹞ *n.* 選民

The *electorate* voted for Mr. Chen.

【先背 elect ﹝ ɪ'lɛkt ﹞ *v.* 選舉】

electronic ﹝ ɪ,lɛk'trɑnɪk ﹞ *adj.* 電子的

Electronic mail has become so popular
that few people bother to write letters
anymore. 【*electronic mail* 電子郵件；
不要與 electric (電的) 搞混】

elegantly ﹝ 'ɛləgəntlɪ ﹞ *adv.* 優雅地

Joanna played the piano *elegantly*.

elevated ﹝ 'ɛlə,vetɪd ﹞ *adj.* 提高的；
地位高的

She holds a more *elevated* position in
the company.

e	+	lev	+ ate	+	d
out	+	*raise*	+ *v.*	+	*adj.*

elevator (ˈɛləˌvetɚ) *n.* 電梯

We have to take the *elevator* to the top of the building instead of walking up the stairs. 【「電扶梯」則是 escalator (ˈɛskəˌletɚ)】

eligible (ˈɛlɪdʒəbḷ) *adj.* 適合的；有資格的

A married person is not *eligible* for dating. 【eligible = suitable】

```
 e   +   lig   + ible
 |        |        |
out + choose +  adj.
```

eliminate (ɪˈlɪməˌnet) *v.* 除去

In order to lose weight, Ricky decided to *eliminate* all sweets from his diet.

```
 e   + limin + ate
 |       |       |
out +  界限  +  v.
```

eloquent ('ɛləkwənt) *adj.* 雄辯的；
口才好的

Everyone was impressed by the *eloquent*
speaker.

```
e  +  loqu  + ent
|       |       |
out + speak + adj.
```

E

elusively (ɪ'lusɪvlɪ) *adv.* 逃避地

The mayor spoke *elusively* about the
situation, so we still don't know what his
real feelings are.【動詞是 elude (逃避)】

```
e  +  lus  + ive + ly
|       |      |      |
out + play + adj. + adv.
```

embassy ('ɛmbəsɪ) *n.* 大使館

There is tight security at most foreign
embassies.【ambassador 是「大使」】

embezzlement 〔 ɪmˈbɛzl̩mənt 〕 *n.*

挪用公款

The prisoner was accused of robbery, assault, *embezzlement* and forgery.

embrace 〔 ɪmˈbres 〕 *v.* 擁抱

Zoo visitors often wish to *embrace* the panda.

【embrace = hug】

em +	brace
|	|
in +	*the arms*

emerge 〔 ɪˈmɝdʒ 〕 *v.* 出現

The chicks *emerged* slowly from the eggs.

e +	merge
|	|
out +	*sink*

emigrant 〔ˈɛməgrənt 〕 *n.*

（移出的）移民

Melody is an *emigrant* from Canada.

【動詞是 emigrate（移出）;「（移入的）移民」
則是 immigrant】

emphasize (ˈɛmfəˌsaɪz) *v.* 強調

The conference *emphasized* the
importance of the microchip industry.
【emphasize = stress = underline】

employee (ˌɛmplɔɪˈi) *n.* 員工

My friend here is an *employee* of a
trading company.【employer 是「老闆」】

enact (ɪnˈækt) *v.* 制定

Next year we will *enact* a
law to limit the sale of
certain drugs.

en + act
| |
in + 法令

encase (ɪnˈkes) *v.* 將…裝進容器

These candies were *encased* in a pretty
box.【encase = en (*in*) + case (箱子)】

enclose (ɪnˈkloz) *v.* (隨函)附寄

We *enclosed* some recent photos of the
baby in the letter.【名詞是 enclosure (附件)】

encounter 〔 ɪn'kaʊntɚ 〕 v. 遭遇

The travelers *encountered* many tough problems but finally solved them.

en + counter
| |
in + against

encourage 〔 ɪn'kɝɪdʒ 〕 v. 鼓勵

Many people worry that the computerized Public Welfare Lottery *encourages* people to gamble rather than work hard to make money. 【先背 courage (勇氣)；它的相反詞是 discourage (使氣餒)】

enforce 〔 ɪn'fors 〕 v. 實施

The problem reflected the government's inability to *enforce* its laws and regulations. 【先背 force (力量)】

engage 〔 ɪn'gedʒ 〕 v. 使參加；從事

A passenger in the next seat tried to *engage* me in conversation.

E

enhance ﹝ ɪn'hæns ﹞ v. 提高；增加

The right accessories will
enhance the beauty of
your dress.

```
en + hance
 |     |
in + high
```

enlarge ﹝ ɪn'lɑrdʒ ﹞ v. 擴大

We plan to *enlarge* the restaurant so that
we can seat another 100 people.

enroll ﹝ ɪn'rol ﹞ v. 登記；入學

25 students have already
enrolled in the class, so it is
almost full. 【*enroll in* 就讀】

```
en + roll
 |     |
in + 名冊
```

ensure ﹝ ɪn'ʃur ﹞ v. 確定

Please *ensure* that all the doors are
locked before you leave.

【ensure（確定）和 insure（投保）發音相同】

enterprise (ˈɛntɚˌpraɪz) *n.* 企業

His successful *enterprise* has netted him millions of dollars a year.

enter	+	prise
|		|
among	+	*seize*

entitle (ɪnˈtaɪtḷ) *v.* 使有資格

She is *entitled* to whatever success she can get.【*be entitled to* 有資格擁有；entitle = en (*in*) + title (頭銜)】

entrance (ˈɛntrəns) *n.* 入口

We used the back *entrance* to the building.【相反詞是 exit (ˈɛgzɪt) *n.* 出口】

entry (ˈɛntrɪ) *n.* 進入

Those who have not paid their club dues by the end of the month will be denied *entry* until they do so.

epidemic〔͵ɛpə'dɛmɪk〕 *n.* 傳染病
adj. 傳染性的

The AIDS *epidemic* has recently reached
a new high.

epi	+	dem	+	ic
among	+	people	+	adj.

equip〔ɪ'kwɪp〕 *v.* 裝備;使配備

A vehicle *equipped* for transporting sick
or injured people is an ambulance.

【它的名詞是 equipment (設備)】

equivalent〔ɪ'kwɪvələnt〕 *adj.* 相等的

A nickel is *equivalent* to five cents.

【*be equivalent to* 等於】

equi	+	val	+	ent
equal	+	worth	+	adj.

escalate ('ɛskə,let) *v.* 逐漸上漲

When supplies of a given product are limited, the price of that product *escalates*.

establish (ə'stæblɪʃ) *v.* 建立

This company was *established* in 1974.

【 establish = found = *set up* 】

E

estate (ə'stet) *n.* 地產

Mr. Chen's real *estate* downtown is worth 3.6 million dollars. 【 *real estate* 不動產 】

estimate ('ɛstə,met) *v.* 估計

I asked the repairman to *estimate* how long it would take him to finish the job.

evaluate (ɪ'vælju,et) *v.* 評估

Speech contestants will be *evaluated* on the basis of fluency and speech content.

【 evaluate = e (*out*) + valu (*value*) + ate (*v.*) 】

eventual〔 ɪˈvɛntʃuəl 〕*adj.* 最後的

Although Mr. Adams is only fifty-five now, we should be prepared for his *eventual* retirement.【eventual = final】

excavation〔ˌɛkskəˈveʃən 〕*n.*
挖掘；開鑿

The *excavation* of the Hsuehshan Tunnel took many months to complete.

【可先背 cave（洞穴）】

ex +	cav	+ at(e) +	ion
out +	hollow +	v. +	n.

excessive〔 ɪkˈsɛsɪv 〕*adj.* 過度的

He accused the police of using *excessive* force to stop the demonstration.

【動詞是 exceed〔ɪkˈsid〕
　　v. 超過】

ex +	cess +	ive
out +	go +	adj.

自我測驗

- [ ] duplicate _____
- [ ] durability _____
- [ ] economical _____
- [ ] elaborate _____
- [ ] elevated _____

- [ ] eligible _____
- [ ] embassy _____
- [ ] emigrant _____
- [ ] enclose _____
- [ ] enforce _____

- [ ] enroll _____
- [ ] entrance _____
- [ ] equip _____
- [ ] estate _____
- [ ] excessive _____

E

1. 缺　點　　　d _drawback_ k
2. 責任；關稅　d _____ y
3. 收　入　　　e _____ s
4. 有效的　　　e _____ e
5. 電子的　　　e _____ c

6. 電　梯　　　e _____ r
7. 挪用公款　　e _____ t
8. 出　現　　　e _____ e
9. 制　定　　　e _____ t
10. 鼓　勵　　　e _____ e

11. 提高；增加　e _____ e
12. 企　業　　　e _____ e
13. 傳染病　　　e _____ c
14. 估　計　　　e _____ e
15. 挖掘；開鑿　e _____ n

E

excursion〔ɪk'skɝʒən〕*n.* 遠足

My roommates and I plan to make an *excursion* to the seaside.

ex	+	curs	+	ion
out	+	run	+	*n.*

E

executive〔ɪg'zɛkjʊtɪv〕*n.* 主管
adj. 行政的;執行的

He is an *executive* in a company.【動詞是 execute〔'ɛksɪ͵kjut〕*v.* 執行;CEO(總裁;執行長)就是 *chief executive officer* 的縮寫】

exhaust〔ɪg'zɔst〕*v.* 使筋疲力盡

They felt quite *exhausted* when they reached the top of the mountain.

exhibition〔͵ɛksə'bɪʃən〕*n.* 展覽會

There will an *exhibition* of her works at the museum next month.

【動詞是 exhibit〔ɪg'zɪbɪt〕*v.* 展示】

existent 〔 ɪgˈzɪstənt 〕 *adj.* 目前的

Under the *existent* circumstances, we should find a solution to the problem as soon as possible.【先背 exist（存在）】

exotic 〔 ɪgˈzɑtɪk 〕 *adj.* 有異國風味的；外來的

There are many *exotic* plants and animals that can only be found in the Amazon.

expansion 〔 ɪkˈspænʃən 〕 *n.* 擴張

The planned *expansion* of the park will provide room for tennis and basketball courts.【動詞是 expand（擴大）】

expect 〔 ɪkˈspɛkt 〕 *v.* 期待

We did not *expect* the performance to be as excellent as it was.

ex	+	pect
|		|
out	+	*look*

expedition〔͵ɛkspɪˈdɪʃən 〕 *n.* 遠征；
探險

China recently made
its first manned
expedition into space.

ex + pedi + tion
| | |
out + foot + n.

expenditure〔 ɪkˈspɛndɪtʃɚ 〕 *n.* 費用

The price included the *expenditure* on
freight.【動詞是 expend（花費），是比
spend 較爲正式的用法】

expense〔 ɪkˈspɛns 〕 *n.* 費用

He paid all the school *expenses* by
himself.【形容詞是 expensive（昂貴的）】

experienced〔 ɪkˈspɪrɪənst 〕 *adj.*
有經驗的

Only an *experienced* actor can memorize
so many lines.【先背 experience（經驗）】

expert ('εksp3t) *n.* 專家

Mechanical engineers are *experts* in
machinery.

【 expert = specialist = professional 】

explanatory (ɪk'splænə,torɪ) *adj.*
說明的

If you don't know the meaning of the
word, you can read the *explanatory*
notes at the bottom of the page.

【 *explanatory notes* 注釋 】

exploration (,εksplə'reʃən) *n.* 探險

Exploration of space is done by
astronauts.

export (ɪks'port) *v.* 出口

We now *export* all kinds of industrial
products.【此字當名詞用時，唸成 ('εksport)】

expressive (ɪk'sprɛsɪv) *adj.* 表情豐富的

A monkey's face is *expressive*.

【動詞是 express（表達），名詞是 expression（表情）】

ex	+ press	+ ive
|	|	|
out +	壓 +	*adj.*

E

expressly (ɪk'sprɛslɪ) *adv.* 明白地

Jack *expressly* told Rose to stop daydreaming.

extend (ɪk'stɛnd) *v.* 延長

We decided to *extend* our lease for another six months.

【名詞 extension 可作「（電話）分機」解】

ex	+ tend
|	|
out +	*stretch*

exterior (ɪk'stɪrɪə) *n.* 外部
adj. 外部的

The *exterior* of the house needs to be painted.【相反詞是 interior (內部;內部的)】

F f

fabric ('fæbrɪk) *n.* 布料
The *fabric* of babies' clothing should be soft.

facility (fə'sɪlətɪ) *n.* 設備;設施
At most schools, *facilities* for learning and recreation are available to students.

fac + il(e) + ity
  | | |
do + adj. + n.

fair (fɛr) *n.* 展覽會 *adj.* 公平的
There will be a book *fair* in January.

FAQ   *n.* 常見問答集
  (= *Frequently Asked Questions*)

Look up the product *FAQs*, and maybe
you can find out what is wrong with
your cell phone.

fare ﹝ fɛr ﹞ *n.* 車資

Can you tell me what the *fare* from
London to Manchester is?

farewell ﹝ˏfɛr'wɛl ﹞ *n.* 告別；告別的話
adj. 告別的

The friends said *farewell* at the airport
and promised to stay in touch.

【*farewell party* 是指「歡送會」】

```
fare + well
 |      |
 go + 良好地（祝人一路順風）
```

F

fascinating 〔'fæsn͵etɪŋ 〕 *adj.* 迷人的

New Zealand has *fascinating* scenery.

favorable 〔'fevərəbl̩ 〕 *adj.* 有利的；
贊許的

Considering the *favorable* response of
the audience, I think we
should give first prize in
the speech contest to Ian.

favor	+	able
贊成	+	*adj.*

F

feature 〔'fitʃə 〕 *n.* 特色；容貌

Beautiful movie actresses with unusual
features—such as dark,
penetrating eyes,
capture attention.

feat	+	ure
make	+	*n.*

federal 〔'fɛdərəl 〕 *adj.* 聯邦的

Most people consider the *Federal*
Bureau of Investigation a mysterious
institution. 【*the Federal Bureau of
Investigation* 聯邦調查局 (= *FBI*)】

fee 〔 fi 〕 *n.* 費用

Dr. Brown charges a high *fee* for his
services.【*charge a fee* 收費】

fiber 〔'faɪbɚ〕 *n.* 纖維

Fresh vegetables have a high *fiber* content.

fiduciary 〔 fɪ'djuʃɪˌɛrɪ 〕 *adj.* 信託的

The trustee was accused of neglecting
his *fiduciary* responsibility when he
mismanaged the heir's assets.【fid 是表
「信任」的字根，如 confident（有自信的）】

file 〔 faɪl 〕 *n.* 文件；檔案 *v.* 歸檔

The bottom drawer of the desk is large
enough to store *files* in.

finalize 〔'faɪnlˌaɪz 〕 *v.* 使完成

Sandy *finalized* her work in time.

fine〔faɪn〕*v.* 對…處以罰金 *n.* 罰金

Will the judge *fine* him heavily?

fixture〔'fɪkstʃɚ〕*n.* 固定物

We're going to remove all of the desks
to another office except this one—it's a
fixture.【先背 fix（使固定）】

flat〔flæt〕*adj.* 平的；沒氣的

Dan laid the map *flat* on the table in order
to see it better.【相反詞是 uneven（不平的）】

flooded〔'flʌdɪd〕*adj.* 淹水的

Many people are still waiting for aid in
the *flooded* districts.【先背 flood（水災）】

flourish〔'flɝɪʃ〕*v.* 繁榮；興隆

The small French restaurant is *flourishing*
and it's always crowded.

【flourish = thrive = prosper】

flu〔flu〕*n.* 流行性感冒

Pam came down with the *flu* and missed a week of school.【flu 是表 flow（流動）的字根；flu = influenza】

fluctuate〔'flʌktʃʊ͵et〕*v.* 波動

The patient's temperature has *fluctuated* between 38 and 40 degrees.

F

fluid〔'fluɪd〕*n.* 流體

Ink is a *fluid* that stains desktops and fingertips.【流體包括 liquid（液體）和 gas（氣體），與它們不同的則是 solid（固體）】

fog〔fɔg〕*n.*（濃）霧

Fog is a cloud near the ground.
【「薄霧」則是 mist】

force〔fors〕*n.* 力量 *v.* 強迫

They *forced* him to sign the document.

forecaster 〔for'kæstɚ〕*n.* 天氣預報者

The *forecaster* said there would be fine weather for the next week.

【動詞是 forecast (預測)】

```
fore  + cast + er
  |       |      |
before + 投擲 +  人
```

F

formation 〔fɔr'meʃən〕*n.* 形成;隊形

The marching band was standing in *formation* on the playing field.

```
form + ation
  |       |
形成  +   n.
```

formerly 〔'fɔrmɚlɪ〕*adv.* 以前

Margaret *formerly* worked in a hospital.

【formerly = previously】

fortunate 〔'fɔrtʃənɪt〕*adj.* 幸運的

Alan was *fortunate* to find a job so quickly.【名詞是 fortune (運氣;財富)】

frequently 〔'frikwəntlɪ〕 *adv.* 經常

The young man is fond of movies, and goes to the theater *frequently*.

【名詞是 frequency (頻繁;頻率);frequently 的相反詞是 seldom 〔'sɛldəm〕 *adv.* 很少】

fringe 〔frɪndʒ〕 *n.* 緣飾;流蘇

Sherry sewed a *fringe* onto the edge of a scarf.

【*fringe benefits* 是指「附加福利;補貼」】

frustrate 〔'frʌstret〕 *v.* 使受挫

If the lesson is too difficult, it will *frustrate* the students.

【名詞是 frustration (挫折)】

frustr	+	ate
|		|
in vain	+	*v.*

FTA   *n.* 自由貿易協定

(= *Free Trade Agreement*)

Taiwan has an *FTA* with Panama.

fuel 〔'fjuəl 〕 *n.* 燃料

A car usually uses gasoline as *fuel*.

fund 〔 fʌnd 〕 *v.* 提供資金   *n.* 資金

How do you plan to *fund* your college
education?【fund 是表 base（基礎）的字根】

furnish 〔'fɝnɪʃ 〕 *v.* 裝置傢俱

My landlord will *furnish* the room with a
sofa and two chairs.【「傢俱」是 furniture】

G g

gateway 〔'get,we 〕 *n.* 大門口

There is a stranger wandering in front
of the *gateway*.

【gateway = gate（大門）+ way（路）】

gauge 〔 gedʒ 〕 *n.* 計量器

We ran out of gas because the *gauge* was
broken.【注意此字的 au 讀 / e /】

gimmick 〔'gɪmɪk 〕 *n.* 花招；噱頭

An advertising *gimmick* is a common marketing method.

【*advertising gimmick* 廣告噱頭】

gradually 〔'grædʒuəlɪ 〕 *adv.* 逐漸地

The snow *gradually* melted.

grassroots 〔'græs'ruts 〕 *adj.*
一般民眾的；基層的

G

The candidates for president are fighting for support at the *grassroots* level.

【grassroots = grass（草）+ roots（根）】

gratitude 〔'grætə,tjud 〕 *n.* 感激

I sent Justine some flowers to express my *gratitude* for her help.

【形容詞是 grateful（感激的）】

grat	+	itude
please	+	*n.*

自我測驗

- [ ] executive   _____
- [ ] exotic   _____
- [ ] expense   _____
- [ ] expert   _____
- [ ] extend   _____

- [ ] fair   _____
- [ ] FAQ   _____
- [ ] favorable   _____
- [ ] fiduciary   _____
- [ ] fine   _____

- [ ] flu   _____
- [ ] forecaster   _____
- [ ] FTA   _____
- [ ] fund   _____
- [ ] grassroots   _____

G

Check List

1. 展覽會　　　e _exhibition_ n
2. 擴　張　　　e _____ n
3. 有經驗的　　e _____ d
4. 說明的　　　e _____ y
5. 表情豐富的　e _____ e

6. 設備；設施　f _____ y
7. 車　資　　　f _____ e
8. 特色；容貌　f _____ e
9. 使完成　　　f _____ e
10. 繁榮；興隆　f _____ h

11. 波　動　　　f _____ e
12. 幸運的　　　f _____ e
13. 經　常　　　f _____ y
14. 裝置傢俱　　f _____ h
15. 感　激　　　g _____ e

G

guarantee 〔͵gærən'ti 〕 v. 保證
　n. 保證書；保證人

Our host *guaranteed* that we would
enjoy the wine. 【guarantee = warrant】

guide 〔 gaɪd 〕 v. 引導　 n. 導遊

She *guided* the visitors around the city.

H h

hacker 〔'hækɚ 〕 n. 駭客

It is important to prevent the intrusion
of *hackers* into the computer network.

handicapped 〔'hændɪ͵kæpt 〕 adj.
殘障的 (= *disabled*)

As she has been *handicapped* all her life,
Terry does not consider having to use a
wheelchair a burden. 【記住 hand (手) 和
cap (帽子)，有些殘障人士會手拿著帽子乞討】

handle (ˈhændḷ) *v.* 處理

The situation is too complicated. I can't
handle it. 【 handle = *deal with* = *cope with* 】

harmonious (harˈmonɪəs) *adj.* 和諧的

It took several hours of practice before
the musicians could produce a
harmonious sound.

【名詞是 harmony (ˈharmənɪ) *n.* 和諧；和聲 】

hassle (ˈhæsḷ) *n.* 麻煩事

It's a *hassle* to go to work on a rainy day.

H

havoc (ˈhævək) *n.* 大破壞

Typhoon Nari caused *havoc* in Taiwan.
【 havoc = destruction = ruin 】

hazard (ˈhæzəd) *n.* 危險

The brave hero faced all *hazards* without
flinching. 【 hazard = danger = risk 】

headlight (ˈhɛdˌlaɪt) *n.* 車前大燈

The Ministry of Transportation and
Communication has ruled that all cars
have to switch their *headlights* on when
they go into the tunnels.

head + light
頭 ＋ 燈

headquarters (ˈhɛdˈkwɔrtɚz) *n. pl.*
總部

This is just a branch office. Our
headquarters are located in Hong Kong.
【headquarters = head + quarters（四分之一）】

heater (ˈhitɚ) *n.* 暖氣機

Please turn on the *heater*.【先背 heat（熱）】

hefty (ˈhɛftɪ) *adj.* 強壯的

Vincent is a *hefty* man and has a perfect
figure.【heft 是作「重量；舉起」解】

hesitate (ˈhɛzəˌtet) *v.* 猶豫

When you see a good
opportunity, don't *hesitate*
to take advantage of it.

hesit + ate
| |
stick + *v.*

【形容詞是 hesitant (猶豫的)】

high-rise (ˈhaɪˈraɪz) *adj.* 高聳的

Taipei 101 is a *high-rise* building.

【high-rise = high (高的) + rise (聳立)；
     high-rise 也可作「高樓大廈」解】

hire (haɪr) *v.* 僱用

That company is *hiring* new people. The
manager will start to interview people
tomorrow. 【相反詞是 fire (解僱)】

homemaker (ˈhomˌmekə) *n.*
家庭主婦 (= *housewife*)

Mrs. Wang is a *homemaker* and her
husband is a doctor.

hook 〔 huk 〕 *n.* 鉤子

Ben hung his jacket on a *hook* behind the door.【虎克船長的英文字就叫作 Hook，因為他的左手是個鉤子；形容詞 hooked 也可作「上癮的」解】

hospitality 〔͵hɑspɪˈtælətɪ 〕 *n.* 慇懃款待

We showed *hospitality* to our Japanese friends when they came to Taiwan.

【*show hospitality to sb.* 熱情款待某人；形容詞是 hospitable (好客的)】

hub 〔 hʌb 〕 *n.* 中心；中樞

Taiwan is presently establishing an Asia-Pacific Regional Operations Center with a view to becoming Asia's world business *hub*.【hub = center】

humid 〔ˈhjumɪd〕 *adj.* 潮濕的

The climate of Taiwan is much more *humid* than that of Alaska.

【humid = wet = moist = damp】

I i

identify 〔aɪˈdɛntəˌfaɪ〕 *v.* 辨認

The police asked the woman to *identify* the man who had stolen her purse.

【名詞是 identity（身分），*ID card*（身分證）就是指 *identity card*】

identi	+ fy
|	|
the same	+ *v.*

illegible 〔ɪˈlɛdʒəbḷ〕 *adj.* 難以辨識的

Mark's handwriting is so *illegible* that I cannot read his letter.

【legible 則是作「易辨認的」解】

il	+ leg	+ ible
|	|	|
not	+ *read*	+ *adj.*

illustrate ('ɪləstret) *v.* 圖解說明

The professor *illustrated* his lecture with diagrams and color slides.

【名詞是 illustration（插圖；實例）】

imitation (ˌɪmə'teʃən) *n.* 模仿

Joe wears his hair long in *imitation* of the rock singer.【*in imitation of* 模仿】

immovable (ɪ'muvəbḷ) *adj.*
不能移動的

There is an *immovable* statue in the center of the square.

impair (ɪm'pɛr) *v.* 損害

Drinking alcohol will *impair* your driving ability.

【repair 是作「修理」解】

im	+	pair
into	+	worse

impeccable 〔 ɪmˈpɛkəbḷ 〕 *adj.* 完美的

The dancer's *impeccable* performance
drew loud applause. 【impeccable = perfect】

impenetrable 〔 ɪmˈpɛnətrəbḷ 〕 *adj.*
不可貫穿的

The bulletproof vest is *impenetrable*.
【先背 penetrate（貫穿）】

implement 〔ˈɪmpləˌmɛnt 〕 *v.* 實行
〔ˈɪmpləmənt 〕 *n.* 用具

As soon as the policy was *implemented*,
crime in the city
dropped dramatically.

im + ple + ment
| | |
in + *fill* + *n.*

implication 〔ˌɪmplɪˈkeʃən 〕 *n.* 暗示

Philip kept silent, with the *implication*
being that he didn't want to continue the
argument. 【形容詞是 implicit（暗示的）】

imply 〔 ɪm'plaɪ 〕 v. 暗示

Are you *implying* that I am
not telling the truth?

```
im + ply
 |     |
in + fold
```

import 〔 ɪm'port 〕 v. 進口

Taiwan *imports* much of its butter and
cheese from New Zealand as it doesn't
produce enough of them.

impose 〔 ɪm'poz 〕 v. 強加

The government *imposes*
a higher tax on the rich
than on the poor.

```
im + pose
 |      |
in + put
```

impress 〔 ɪm'prɛs 〕 v. 使印象深刻

We were greatly *impressed* by his speech.

【 *be greatly impressed by*… 對…印象深刻 】

in charge of 負責管理

The Quality Control Department is *in
charge of* inspecting goods for defects.

in line with 與…一致

Ben's idea is *in line with* my proposal.

【 *in line with* = *in agreement with* 】

inadequate 〔 ɪn'ædəkwɪt 〕 *adj.* 不足的

The budget is *inadequate* for a trip to

Italy.

in	+ ad +	equ	+ ate
|	|	|	|
not +	*to* +	*equal* +	*adj.*

inauguration 〔 ɪnˌɔgjə'reʃən 〕 *n.*
開幕典禮；就職典禮

The *inauguration* of the new branch will

take place on August 1.

【 先背 augur（預言）】

incentive 〔 ɪn'sɛntɪv 〕 *n.* 誘因；動機

The bank is offering *incentives* to people

who sign up for their new credit card.

increment〔'ɪnkrəmənt〕 *n.* 增額

Your salary will be adjusted by an annual *increment* of \$50.

in +	cre +	ment
in +	grow +	*n.*

indecisive〔,ɪndɪ'saɪsɪv〕 *adj.*
優柔寡斷的

We have lost faith in the *indecisive* leader.

indicate〔'ɪndə,ket〕 *v.* 指出

He *indicated* the fire station on the map for me. 【indicate = *point out*】

individually〔,ɪndə'vɪdʒʊəlɪ〕 *adv.*
個別地

The candies are wrapped *individually*, each one in a different color of paper.

in +	divid +	ual +	ly
not +	divide +	adj. +	adv. （不能再分割地）

industrious ﹝ ɪn'dʌstrɪəs ﹞ *adj.* 勤勞的

There is a bonus system at the factory to reward the most *industrious* workers.

【不要跟 industrial（工業的）的意思搞混】

inefficient ﹝ ˌɪnə'fɪʃənt ﹞ *adj.* 無效率的

Washing dishes by hand is an *inefficient* use of time.

【相反詞是 efficient（有效率的）】

infection ﹝ ɪn'fɛkʃən ﹞ *n.* 感染

The doctor said I had a mild *infection* and gave me some pills to take.

infestation ﹝ ˌɪnfɛs'teʃən ﹞ *n.* 橫行

An *infestation* of pests made for a bad crop of cabbages.

in	+ fest	+ ation
against	strike	*n.*

infinite ('ɪnfənɪt) *adj.* 無限的

Even the most powerful telescope cannot tell us everything about the *infinite* universe.【fin 是表 end（結束）的字根，如 final（最後的）; infinite = limitless; 相反詞是 finite ('faɪnaɪt) *adj.* 有限的】

inform (ɪn'fɔrm) *v.* 通知

As his itinerary had been changed, he *informed* the front desk that he would leave early.【inform = notify】

infrastructure ('ɪnfrə,strʌktʃɚ) *n.* 基礎建設

Roadways and utility services make up part of a city's *infrastructure*.

```
infra  + structure
  |         |
below +   建築物
```

initiative〔 ɪ'nɪʃɪˏetɪv 〕 *n.* 主動

If you want to make new friends, you should take the *initiative* instead of just waiting for others to talk to you.

【*take the initiative* 採取主動；先背

initial〔 ɪ'nɪʃəl 〕*adj.* 最初的】

injure〔'ɪndʒɚ 〕*v.* 傷害

Don't hold the knife like that or you may *injure* yourself.【名詞是 injury（傷）】

innovative〔'ɪnoˏvetɪv 〕*adj.* 創新的

Innovative ideas are necessary to make the business a success.

in	+ nov	+ ative
in	+ new	+ adj.

inquiry〔 ɪn'kwaɪrɪ 〕*n.* 詢問

I made an *inquiry* about the details of the journey.【*make an inquiry* 詢問】

insect ('ɪnsɛkt) *n.* 昆蟲

A butterfly is an *insect*.

【昆蟲的身體一節一節的,像
被切成很多 section (部分)】

```
in  + sect
 |      |
into + cut
```

inspect (ɪn'spɛkt) *v.* 檢查

The factory will be *inspected* today to
make sure that it is a
safe workplace.

【 inspect = examine 】

```
in  + spect
 |      |
into + look
```

installment (ɪn'stɔlmənt) *n.*
分期付款的錢

I just paid the last *installment* on the
refrigerator; now we own it.

【先背 install (安裝),分期付款就像在安裝
軟體,要一步一步慢慢來】

institute ('ɪnstə‚tjut) *n.* 協會;機構

The millionaire founded an *institute*
dedicated to helping the poor.

自我測驗

- [ ] handicapped   _____
- [ ] hazard   _____
- [ ] headquarters   _____
- [ ] high-rise   _____
- [ ] hook   _____

- [ ] identify   _____
- [ ] illustrate   _____
- [ ] implement   _____
- [ ] imply   _____
- [ ] incentive   _____

- [ ] increment   _____
- [ ] industrious   _____
- [ ] infrastructure   _____
- [ ] innovative   _____
- [ ] inspect   _____

I

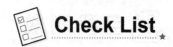

1. 保　證	g _guarantee_	e
2. 和諧的	h _____	s
3. 暖氣機	h _____	r
4. 猶　豫	h _____	e
5. 慇懃款待	h _____	y
6. 潮濕的	h _____	d
7. 不能移動的	i _____	e
8. 不可貫穿的	i _____	e
9. 強　加	i _____	e
10. 不足的	i _____	e
11. 指　出	i _____	e
12. 感　染	i _____	n
13. 通　知	i _____	m
14. 詢　問	i _____	y
15. 分期付款的錢	i _____	t

I

instruction (ɪn'strʌkʃən) *n.* 指示

The *instruction* he gave was not clear.

integrity (ɪn'tɛgrətɪ) *n.* 正直；廉潔

When money began to disappear from
the account, we questioned the *integrity*
of the accountant.

【 integrity = honesty 】

in +	tegr	+ ity
not +	touch +	*n.*

intellectual (ˌɪntḷ'ɛktʃʊəl) *adj.* 智力的

Nutrition is important for children's
intellectual development.

intended (ɪn'tɛndɪd) *adj.* 預期的

The promotional activity had the
intended effect. 【tend、tens、tent 都是
表 stretch (伸展) 的字根】

intensely (ɪn'tɛnslɪ) *adv.* 強烈地

Susan was *intensely* annoyed by the
noise. 【先背 tense (緊張的)】

intentional 〔ɪn'tɛnʃənḷ〕 *adj.* 故意的

Thomas used an *intentional* insult to break his girlfriend's heart.

【動詞是 intend（打算），名詞是 intention（意圖）; intentional = deliberate】

interact 〔͵ɪntɚ'ækt〕 *v.* 相互作用

These two chemicals will *interact* and produce a gas with a terrible smell.

【interact = inter (*between*) + act（行動）】

interchangeable 〔͵ɪntɚ'tʃendʒəbḷ〕

adj. 可替換的

"Baby" and "infant" are *interchangeable* words.【先背 change（替換）】

intercom 〔'ɪntɚ͵kɑm〕 *n.* 對講機

Inside a Taipei MRT train, you can use an *intercom* to contact the driver in an emergency.【com 是 communication（溝通）】

interest (ˈɪntrɪst) *n.* 興趣；利益；利息

The *interest* that I earn from the bonds in the bank is the money that I make on my capital.

interfere (ˌɪntəˈfɪr) *v.* 干涉

I tried to help my friends resolve their argument, but they told me not to *interfere*.

inter	+	fere
|		|
between	+	*strike*

intermittently (ˌɪntəˈmɪtn̩tlɪ) *adv.* 間歇地

The fountain spouts out water *intermittently*.【mit 是表 send (送) 的字根】

intern (ˈɪntɝn) *n.* 實習醫師

A medical student usually spends two years in a hospital as an *intern*.

interrupt 〔͵ɪntə'rʌpt〕v. 打斷

She rudely *interrupted* our conversation.

【interrupt = inter (*between*) + rupt (*break*)】

inundate 〔'ɪnʌn͵det〕v. (如洪水般) 湧到

After the release of their new product, the company was soon *inundated* with orders. 【inundate = in + un + date (日期)】

invasion 〔ɪn'veʒən〕n. 入侵

The Chinese built the Great Wall to protect themselves from *invasion*.

【動詞是 invade (入侵)】

inventive 〔ɪn'vɛntɪv〕adj. 有發明才能的

in + vent + ive
| | |
in + come + adj.

The *inventive* genius created several amazing devices.

inventory 141 **invoice**

inventory ('ɪnvən,torɪ) *n.* 存貨清單

Count every item so that our *inventory* will be accurate. 〔inventory = *stock list*〕

investigate (ɪn'vɛstə,get) *v.* 調查

The police are *investigating* the disappearance of the painting from the museum. 〔investigate = invest (投資) + i + gate (大門)〕

invisible (ɪn'vɪzəbḷ) *adj.* 看不見的

Ultraviolet rays are *invisible* to the naked eye.

in	+ vis	+ ible
not	+ *see*	+ *adj.*

invoice ('ɪnvɔɪs) *n.* 發貨單;發票

The company included an *invoice* in the package that told me what goods were inside. 〔invoice = in + voice (聲音)〕

involve〔 ɪn'vɑlv 〕v. 使牽涉

I am sorry to have
involved you in this matter.

in + volve
| |
in + roll

irresponsible〔 ˌɪrɪ'spɑnsəbḷ 〕adj.
不負責任的

The *irresponsible* mother left her child
alone in the house for three days.

irritation〔 ˌɪrə'teʃən 〕n. 激怒；生氣

Henry couldn't hide his *irritation* at their
rudeness.【動詞是 irritate（激怒）】

issue〔'ɪʃu 〕n. 議題 v. 發行

Unemployment is an important *issue*.
【issue 也可指「（雜誌的）…期」】

itinerary〔 aɪ'tɪnəˌrɛrɪ 〕n. 行程

The *itinerary* for our trip was set by the
travel agency.【it 是表 go（去）的字根，
如 transit（通過）】

J j

【J / K】

janitor 〔'dʒænətɚ 〕 *n.* 管理員

The *janitor* comes to clean our classroom
every day.

jani	+ tor
|	|
Janus (門神)	+ 人

jumble 〔'dʒʌmbḷ 〕 *n.* 雜亂的一堆

There was a *jumble* of dirty clothes in
Flora's room.

jurisprudence 〔ˌdʒʊrɪs'prudn̩s 〕 *n.*
法律學

All law students must take classes in
jurisprudence so that they will
understand the theory behind the law
they practice.

【先背 jury (陪審團)】

juris	+ prudence
|	|
law	+ 慎重

J

K k

keynote address *n.* （政黨的）基本方針演說

The Democrat gained fame after he gave the *keynote address* at a political convention.【keynote 是作「基本方針」解，而 address 在這裡是作「演說」解】

knowledgeable〔'nɑlɪdʒəbḷ〕*adj.* 有知識的

Mr. Williams is a very *knowledgeable* person in this field.

L l

label〔'lebḷ〕*n.* 標籤

According to the *label*, this shirt is made of cotton.【label = tag】

labor 〔'lebɚ〕 *n.* 勞動;勞工

The farmer took a rest from his *labor*.

laboratory 〔'læbrə,torɪ〕 *n.* 實驗室

The student conducted experiments in chemistry in the *laboratory*.

【-ory 是表「地方」的字尾】

landscape 〔'lændskep〕 *n.* 風景

We took several photographs of the beautiful *landscape* of southern France.

launch 〔lɔntʃ〕 *v.* 發射;發售(新產品)

The rocket will be *launched* on Friday.

laundry 〔'lɔndrɪ〕 *n.* 要洗的衣服

We always do the *laundry* on Tuesday and the shopping on Wednesday.

【*do the laundry* 洗衣服】

L

lax 〔 læks 〕 *adj.* 散漫的

Vivian's *lax* attitude to work angered her boss.【相反詞是 strict (嚴格的)】

leadership 〔'lidɚʃɪp 〕 *n.* 領導

Under Connie's *leadership*, our team won the championship.【動詞是 lead (領導)】

leaflet 〔'liflɪt 〕 *n.* 傳單

The clerk is distributing *leaflets* to passersby.【先背 leaf (葉子)；leaflet = flier 】

leak 〔 lik 〕 *v.* 漏出

There was a hole in my cup and the coffee *leaked* all over the table.

lease 〔 lis 〕 *v.* 租   *n.* 租約

We will *lease* your house for one year.

leather 〔ˈlɛðɚ〕 *n.* 皮革

Alice's wallet is made of genuine *leather*.

【*genuine leather* 眞皮】

lecture 〔ˈlɛktʃɚ〕 *n.* 演講

Please turn your cell phones
off before the *lecture* begins.

【lecture = speech】

lect	+ ure
read +	*n.*

legislation 〔ˌlɛdʒɪsˈleʃən〕 *n.* 立法

It is too late in the year for *legislation* to
pass in Congress.

【legislator 則是
「立法委員」】

legis +	lat	+ ion
law +	*bring* +	*n.*

legitimate 〔lɪˈdʒɪtəmɪt〕 *adj.* 合法的

The owner was operating a *legitimate*
gun shop because he had all the right
permits. 【legitimate = legal = lawful】

L

leisure 〔'liʒɚ 〕 *adj.* 空閒的　*n.* 空閒

I am so busy that I have no *leisure* time for sport.

libel 〔'laɪbḷ 〕 *n.* 誹謗（罪）

The subject of that scandalous book brought *libel* charges against its author.

```
lib  +  el
 |        |
book + small （在書裡面寫傷害別人名聲的事）
```

lift 〔 lɪft 〕 *v.* 舉起；抱起

The mother *lifts* her baby up gently.

limousine 〔'lɪməˌzin , ˌlɪmə'zin 〕 *n.*
大型高級轎車

At the Oscar ceremony, many movie stars arrived in *limousines* and walked down the red carpet. 【limousine = limo 〔'lɪmo 〕】

litter (ˈlɪtɚ) *v.* 亂丟垃圾

There is a fine for *littering* in the park,
so be sure to place your trash
in the trash can.

loan (lon) *n.* 貸款

Not being able to afford the cost of the
car, they asked the bank for a *loan*.

lobby (ˈlɑbɪ) *n.* 大廳　*v.* 遊說

You will find the elevators in the *lobby*
of the building.

lodge (lɑdʒ) *v.* 住宿　*n.* 小屋

You will enjoy staying at a *lodge* in the
mountains.

lucrative (ˈlukrətɪv) *adj.* 可獲利的

The company just won a very *lucrative*
contract.【lucrative = profitable】

L

luggage (ˊlʌgɪdʒ) *n.* 行李

Bob brought two pieces of *luggage* on the trip.【luggage = baggage，都是不可數名詞】

lull (lʌl) *v.* 使入睡

Mary *lulled* her baby to sleep.
【lullaby 是「搖籃曲」，唸作 (ˊlʌləˌbaɪ)】

luxury (ˊlʌkʃərɪ) *n.* 奢侈品

I can't afford to spend the money on *luxuries*.【形容詞是 luxurious (奢侈的)；相反詞是 necessity (nəˋsɛsətɪ) *n.* 必需品】

M m

maid (med) *n.* 女傭

The *maid* prepares meals for her boss every day.

maintenance ﹝'mentənəns ﹞ *n.* 維修

Without the proper *maintenance*, your car will not last long.【注意此字的發音；動詞是 maintain（維持），唸作﹝men'ten﹞】

malfunction ﹝mæl'fʌŋkʃən ﹞ *n.* 故障

The fax machine had a *malfunction* and we have not received any faxes since yesterday.【先背 function（功能），mal- 是表 badly（壞）的字首】

manageable ﹝'mænɪdʒəbḷ ﹞ *adj.* 能處理的

Melissa's job is tough but *manageable*.

mandatory ﹝'mændə,torɪ ﹞ *adj.* 義務性的

In Taiwan, it is *mandatory* for every child to attend school until he is 16.【mandatory = mand (*order*) + at(e) (*v.*) + ory (*adj.*)】

自我測驗

- [ ] intensely   _____
- [ ] interact   _____
- [ ] intern   _____
- [ ] inundate   _____
- [ ] inventory   _____

- [ ] issue   _____
- [ ] janitor   _____
- [ ] label   _____
- [ ] launch   _____
- [ ] leaflet   _____

- [ ] legislation   _____
- [ ] leisure   _____
- [ ] lodge   _____
- [ ] luxury   _____
- [ ] maintenance   _____

Check List

1. 指　示	i _instruction_ n
2. 對講機	i ＿＿＿＿＿ m
3. 干　涉	i ＿＿＿＿＿ e
4. 有發明才能的	i ＿＿＿＿＿ e
5. 發貨單；發票	i ＿＿＿＿＿ e
6. 使牽涉	i ＿＿＿＿＿ e
7. 雜亂的一堆	j ＿＿＿＿＿ e
8. 勞動；勞工	l ＿＿＿＿＿ r
9. 要洗的衣服	l ＿＿＿＿＿ y
10. 漏　出	l ＿＿＿＿＿ k
11. 皮　革	l ＿＿＿＿＿ r
12. 舉起；抱起	l ＿＿＿＿＿ t
13. 貸　款	l ＿＿＿＿＿ n
14. 行　李	l ＿＿＿＿＿ e
15. 故　障	m ＿＿＿＿＿ n

mankind 〔 mæn'kaɪnd 〕 *n.* 人類

Mankind did not exist ten million years ago. 【mankind = *human beings*】

manual 〔'mænjʊəl〕*adj.* 手工的   *n.* 手冊

I have read the *manual*, but I still don't understand how to operate this machine.

【manual = handbook】

```
manu +  al
 |       |
hand  + adj.
```

manufacturer 〔,mænjə'fæktʃərɚ 〕 *n.*
製造業者；廠商

Hoping to increase business, the *manufacturers* advertised their products on the radio. 【動詞是 manufacture（製造）】

manuscript 〔'mænjə,skrɪpt 〕 *n.* 手稿

The publishers found the *manuscript* of Carrie's report. 【script 是表「寫」的字根】

marginal 〔'mɑrdʒɪnḷ〕 *adj.* 邊際的

Marginal benefit is the change in total benefit resulting from an action.

【名詞是 margin（邊緣；邊際）】

maritime 〔'mærəˌtaɪm〕 *adj.* 海運的；沿海的

The people who live near the sea are called "*maritime* people".

【mari 是表 sea（海）的字根】

marketing 〔'mɑrkɪtɪŋ〕 *n.* 行銷

Marketing plays an important role in business.【先背 market（市場）】

master 〔'mæstɚ〕 *n.* 主人；大師
v. 精通

If you study hard, you can *master* English.

maximum (ˈmæksəməm) *n.* 最大量

She types a *maximum* of seventy words per minute.【相反詞是 minimum (最小量)】

means (minz) *n.* 方法;手段

My brother believes that going for a daily swim is the best *means* of staying in shape.

【此字單複數同形;means = way = method】

mechanic (məˈkænɪk) *n.* 技工

Mr. Brown is a good *mechanic*.

【mechanic = mechan (*machine*) + ic (人)】

medical (ˈmɛdɪkḷ) *adj.* 醫學的

Dr. Peterson has a Ph.D. in history; he is not a *medical* doctor.

$$
\begin{array}{c}
\text{med} + \text{ical} \\
| \qquad | \\
\textit{heal} + \textit{adj.}
\end{array}
$$

memorandum 〔͵mɛmə'rændəm〕 *n.*
備忘錄（= *memo*）

Alex wrote a *memorandum* to do homework so that he would not forget.

【memor 是表 remember（記得）的字根】

mention 〔'mɛnʃən〕 *v.* 提到

Did you *mention* the party to Jill? She seems to know all about it.

merchandise 〔'mɝtʃən͵daɪz〕 *n.* 商品

The variety of *merchandise* in the store awed us.【merc 是表 trade（交易）的字根，merchant 是指「商人」; merchandise = goods】

merge 〔mɝdʒ〕 *v.* 合併

This small company *merged* with a large international company.

【相反詞是 separate 〔'sɛpə͵ret〕 *v.* 使分開】

minimize 〔'mɪnə,maɪz〕 v. 使減到最小

How can we *minimize* the possibility of being late?【相反詞 maximize（使達到最大）】

miscellaneous 〔,mɪsḷ'enɪəs〕 adj. 種類繁多的

I still have a few *miscellaneous* items to pick up from my old apartment, and then I will be completely moved out.

【此字源自於 mix（混合）】

moisture 〔'mɔɪstʃɚ〕 n. 濕氣；水分

It is important to control the *moisture* of the soil if you want this plant to grow well.【先背 moist（潮濕的）】

mop 〔mɑp〕 v. 用拖把拖（地板）

I *mopped* the floor every day.「掃」是 sweep，「用吸塵器打掃」是 vacuum】

motion sickness *n.* 暈車 (船、機)

Elle always has *motion sickness*, so she takes a medicine before taking a bus.

motivate (ˈmotəˌvet) *v.* 激勵

In order to *motivate* him, Dan's parents promised to buy him a new bike if he improved his grades.

【motive 是指「動機」】

motiv + ate
| |
move + *v.*

multinational (ˌmʌltɪˈnæʃənl̩) *adj.* 多國的；跨國的

Microsoft is a *multinational* company.

【multi- 是表 many (很多的) 的字首】

mutually (ˈmjutʃʊəlɪ) *adv.* 互相地

It would be best if we met at a *mutually* convenient place.

N n

【N/O】

navigate 〔'nævə,get 〕 *v.* 航行（於）

Sailors used to *navigate* the seas by looking at the stars.

nav	+	ig	+ ate
ship	+	drive	+ *v.*

necessitate 〔 nə'sɛsə,tet 〕 *v.* 使成為必要

Making a mistake does not *necessitate* your offering an excuse.

【先背 necessary 〔'nɛsə,sɛrɪ 〕 *adj.* 必要的】

negotiation 〔 nɪ,goʃɪ'eʃən 〕 *n.* 談判

The two countries conducted peace *negotiations* to end the war.

neg	+	oti	+ at(e)	+ ion
not	+	leisure	+ *v.*	+ *n.*

norm〔 nɔrm 〕*n.* 標準;規範

No one should violate the social *norms*.

【形容詞是 normal(正常的)】

notify〔'notəˏfaɪ〕*v.* 通知

If you continue to be absent from your classes, we will *notify* your parents.

【not 是表 know(知道)的字根】

notoriety〔ˏnotə'raɪətɪ〕*n.* 惡名昭彰

The mayor earned *notoriety* for taking bribes.【形容詞是 notorious〔no'torɪəs〕*adj.* 惡名昭彰的】

numerical〔nju'mɛrɪkl̩〕*adj.* 數字的

The papers were filed in *numerical* order.

【***in numerical order*** 按數字的順序】

numer	+	ical
number	+	*adj.*

O o

objection ﹝ əb'dʒɛkʃən ﹞ *n.* 反對

Teenagers usually make an *objection* to what their parents say.

obscure ﹝ əb'skjʊr ﹞ *adj.* 模糊的

We watched the ship sail away until it was nothing but an *obscure* spot in the distance.

ob	+	scure
over	+	covered

observantly ﹝ əb'zɜvəntlɪ ﹞ *adv.*
小心遵守地

Judy followed the instructions *observantly* lest she break the machine.

【先背 observe ﹝ əb'zɜv ﹞ *v.* 遵守】

obstacle ('ɑbstəkḷ) *n.* 阻礙

George found it difficult to get around in a wheelchair because there were so many *obstacles* in his path. 【 obstacle = barrier 】

ob	+	sta	+	cle
against	+	*stand*	+	*n.*

obstruct (əb'strʌkt) *v.* 妨礙；堵塞

After the storm, fallen trees *obstructed* the streets and traffic was terribly congested.

ob	+	struct
against	+	*build*

occupation (,ɑkjə'peʃən) *n.* 職業

His *occupation* was selling vegetables in the market. 【 occupation = job 】

occur 〔ə'kɝ〕 v. 發生

I didn't see the accident *occur*, but I was there when the police arrived.

【 occur = happen = *take place* 】

offer 〔'ɔfɚ〕 v. 提供

He *offered* me a better job.

off-season 〔'ɔf'sizən〕 n. 淡季

In the *off-season*, there are few people at Disneyland. 【相反詞是 season (旺季)】

omit 〔o'mɪt〕 v. 遺漏

Don't *omit* his name from the list.

o	+ mit
away	+ send

on duty 上班

Steve was fired because he went on a date while *on duty*. 【相反詞是 *off duty* (下班)】

operation [ˌɑpəˈreʃən] *n.* 手術

I had an *operation* on my heart.

【*have an operation* 接受手術】

optimistic [ˌɑptəˈmɪstɪk] *adj.* 樂觀的

City residents are *optimistic* that transportation will be improved in the near future. 【相反詞是 pessimistic (悲觀的)】

option [ˈɑpʃən] *n.* 選擇

After graduating from high school, every student has the *option*

of beginning a career or attending college.

【option = choice】

oral [ˈɔrəl] *adj.* 口頭的

Students will have to take an *oral* exam as well as a written one.

【有個牙膏品牌叫作 Oral B (歐樂 B)】

ordinance ('ɔrdn̩əns) *n.* 法令

A state *ordinance* prohibits the sale of
cigarettes to minors.

ordin	+	ance
order	+	*n.*

oriental (,orɪ'ɛntl̩) *adj.* 東方的

Oriental food is popular worldwide.

【「西方的」則是 occidental (,ɑksə'dɛntl̩)】

oriented ('orɪ,ɛntɪd) *adj.* …取向的

You must be service *oriented* if you want
to succeed in the hotel and restaurant
business.【先背 orient (東方；定…的方位)】

out of place 不適當的

Using cell phone or chatting loudly is
out of place at a concert.

【 *out of place* = improper = unfitting 】

outline (ˈaʊtˌlaɪn) *n.* 大綱

My teacher suggested that I write an *outline* of my main ideas before I try to write the research paper.

【 outline = out (外面的) + line (線); outline = summary 】

overall (ˈovəˌɔl) *adj.* 全面的

Our army won an *overall* victory in this campaign. 【overalls 是指「工作服」】

overdue (ˈovəˈdju) *adj.* 逾期的

His credit card bill is *overdue*, and now he has to pay a high rate of interest.

【 overdue = over (超過) + due (到期的)】

overhead (ˈovəˌhɛd) *adj.* 經常的

The report shows that *overhead* expenses are too high. 【*overhead expenses* 經常費用】

overlook〔͵ovɚ'lʊk〕v. 忽略

Rachel *overlooked* this book when she
returned the others to the library.
【 overlook = miss = forget 】

overrule〔͵ovɚ'rul〕v. 推翻；駁回

Congress *overruled* the proposal.
【先背 rule（規則；統治）】

oversight〔'ovɚ͵saɪt〕n. 疏忽

Not inviting the Smiths to the wedding
was a terrible *oversight*.【先背 sight（視力）】

oversized〔'ovɚ'saɪzd〕adj. 特大的

Hank was so hungry that he ordered an
oversized meal.【 oversized = oversize 】

overtime〔'ovɚ͵taɪm〕n. 加班

Brian had done *overtime* until midnight
and he was worn out.【 *do overtime* 加班 】

自我測驗

- [ ] manual _____
- [ ] maritime _____
- [ ] means _____
- [ ] memorandum _____
- [ ] miscellaneous _____

- [ ] motivate _____
- [ ] navigate _____
- [ ] norm _____
- [ ] observantly _____
- [ ] occupation _____

- [ ] on duty _____
- [ ] optimistic _____
- [ ] out of place _____
- [ ] overhead _____
- [ ] overlook _____

O

O

1. 人　類　　　　m _mankind_ d
2. 行　銷　　　　m _____ g
3. 最大量　　　　m _____ m
4. 商　品　　　　m _____ e
5. 濕氣；水分　　m _____ e

6. 互相地　　　　m _____ y
7. 談　判　　　　n _____ n
8. 通　知　　　　n _____ y
9. 模糊的　　　　o _____ e
10. 妨礙；堵塞　　o _____ t

11. 淡　季　　　　o _____ n
12. 口頭的　　　　o _____ l
13. 東方的　　　　o _____ l
14. 逾期的　　　　o _____ e
15. 加　班　　　　o _____ e

overtly 〔 oˊvɝtlɪ 〕 *adv.* 公然地

To our surprise, Jack revolted against the teacher *overtly*. 【相反詞 covertly (秘密地)】

overwhelming 〔ˏovɚˊhwɛlmɪŋ 〕 *adj.* 壓倒性的

Under Mark's guidance the company has enjoyed *overwhelming* success.

P p

【P/Q】

pace 〔 pes 〕 *n.* 步調

Becky walked through the store at such a fast *pace* that I couldn't keep up with her.

participate 〔 parˊtɪsəˏpet 〕 *v.* 參加

The others are playing cards, but I decided not to *participate*.

parti	+ cip	+ ate
part	+ take	+ v.

partnership ('partnɚ,ʃɪp) *n.* 合夥關係

Their *partnership* ended when they could not agree on the best way to run the business.【先背 partner (夥伴)】

patronage ('petrənɪdʒ) *n.* 贊助；惠顧

The shopkeeper expressed his thanks to customers for their *patronage*.

【先背 patron (贊助者；主顧)】

```
patr  + on + age
 |       |     |
father + 人 + n.
```

paycheck ('pe'tʃɛk) *n.* 薪水支票

The factory went bankrupt and none of the workers could cash their *paycheck*.

【paycheck = pay (薪水) + check (支票)】

peace (pis) *n.* 和平

Both warring nations longed for *peace*.

pedestrian ﹝ pə'dɛstrɪən ﹞ *n.* 行人

It was reckless of the *pedestrian* to try to cross the street against the light. 【ped 是表 foot (腳) 的字根，如 pedal (踏板)】

P

peer ﹝ pɪr ﹞ *n.* 同儕   *v.* 凝視；盯著看

Grandmother *peered* through her glasses at the stranger.

penalty ﹝'pɛnḷtɪ ﹞ *n.* 刑罰

What is the *penalty* for speeding on this road? 【penalty = punishment】

pen	+	al	+	ty
|		|		|
punish	+	*adj.*	+	*n.*

pending ﹝'pɛndɪŋ ﹞ *adj.* 未決定的；待解決的

Last year, the court had 500 *pending* cases.

pend	+	ing
|		|
hang	+	*adj.*

pension 〔'pɛnʃən 〕 *n.* 退休金

My father is retired and
lives on his *pension*.

pens	+	ion
weigh	+	*n.*

perception 〔 pɚ'sɛpʃən 〕 *n.* 知覺；看法

Your prejudice against female politicians
is affecting your *perception* of the
candidate's speech.

【動詞是 perceive 〔 pɚ'siv 〕 *v.* 察覺】

performance 〔 pɚ'fɔrməns 〕 *n.* 表演

The actor's *performance* was worthy of
an Oscar.【動詞是 perform (表演)】

persecution 〔ˌpɝsɪ'kjuʃən 〕 *n.* 迫害

The Jews suffered terrible *persecution*
during World War II.

per	+	secut	+	ion
through	+	*follow*	+	*n.*

personnel 〔͵pɝsn̩'ɛl 〕 *n.* 全體職員

Airline *personnel* can purchase flight
tickets at reduced prices.

【*personnel manager* 則是「人事主任」】

persuade 〔 pɚ'swed 〕 *v.* 說服

The salesman *persuaded* me to buy the
TV by offering me a free gift.

pesticide 〔'pɛstɪ͵saɪd 〕 *n.* 殺蟲劑

The use of *pesticide* may result in a
greenhouse effect.

【suicide 則是「自殺」】

pest + icide
|　　　|
害蟲 + *kill*

pharmaceutical 〔͵fɑrmə'sutɪk̩l 〕 *adj.*
製藥的

Bayer is one of the biggest
pharmaceutical companies in the world.

【先背 pharmacy（藥房）】

phone log *n.* 電話記錄日誌

You can use a *phone log* to keep track of the calls you have made.

【log 在這裡是作「記錄；日誌」解】

pile〔paɪl〕*n.* 堆

He puts the fruit in *piles* under the tree.

pipe〔paɪp〕*n.* 管子；煙斗

I handed my father a *pipe*.

platform〔'plæt,fɔrm〕*n.* 講台；月台

The students stood on a *platform* when they gave their speeches.

【platform = plat (*flat*) + form (形狀)】

plenary〔'plinərɪ〕*adj.* 全體出席的

We will elect a new director of the board at the *plenary* meeting next week.

plen	+	ary
full	+	*adj.*

plot 〔 plɑt 〕 *n.* 情節

The movie is so complicated that I cannot follow the *plot*.【plot = *story line*】

pneumonia 〔 nju'monjə 〕 *n.* 肺炎

SARS is also called "atypical *pneumonia*" in China.【注意字首的 p 不發音】

population 〔 ˌpɑpjə'leʃən 〕 *n.* 人口

China has a large *population*.

【popul 是表 people（人）的字根】

portable 〔'portəbl̩ 〕 *adj.* 手提的

Lucy's parents gave her a *portable* CD player for her birthday.

port	+	able
|		|
carry	+	*adj.*

portion 〔'porʃən 〕 *n.* 部分

As it was my birthday, Mother gave me the largest *portion* of the cake.

position ﹝ pəˈzɪʃən ﹞ *n.* 位置

Someone removed the
book from its *position*
on the shelf.

posit + ion
| |
put + *n.*

possess ﹝ pəˈzɛs ﹞ *v.* 擁有

He *possessed* great wisdom.

postage ﹝ ˈpostɪdʒ ﹞ *n.* 郵資

Postage and insurance for the package
amounted to three hundred dollars.

【 postage = post (郵件) + age 】

postpone ﹝ postˈpon ﹞ *v.* 延期

We decided to *postpone* the class reunion
until after the New Year holiday.

【 postpone = *put off* 】

potential〔pə'tɛnʃəl〕adj. 有潛力的；可能的

We are seen as *potential* consumers by advertisers.

potent	+ ial
|	|
powerful	+ *adj.*

P

poverty line   n. 貧窮線

Most of the people in this country live below the *poverty line*.

【poverty〔'pɑvətɪ〕n. 貧窮】

practical〔'præktɪkḷ〕adj. 實際的

Although he studied management in college, John does not have any *practical* experience.

【相反詞是 theoretical〔,θiə'rɛtɪkḷ〕adj. 理論的】

praise〔prez〕v. n. 稱讚

My teacher always *praises* me.

【此字源自 price，給予好的評價，即「稱讚」；相反詞是 criticize〔'krɪtə,saɪz〕v. 批評】

precedent〔'prɛsədənt〕n. 先例

There is no *precedent* for such a discount.

pre	+ cede	+ (e)nt
before	+ go	+ n.

predecessor〔ˌprɛdɪ'sɛsɚ〕n. 前輩

The policy was made and implemented by his *predecessor*.【相反詞是 successor〔sək'sɛsɚ〕n. 後繼者;繼承人】

preference〔'prɛfərəns〕n. 比較喜歡

His *preference* is for coffee rather than tea.【先背 prefer〔prɪ'fɝ〕v. 比較喜歡】

premier〔'primɪɚ〕n. 首相

The *premier* took responsibility for the failed policy and resigned his post.

【premier = prem (*first*) + ier (人)】

premise ('prɛmɪs) *n.* 前提;(*pl.*) 房產

The high school operates on the *premise* that students should be taught values.

pre	+ mise
before	+ send

prescription (prɪ'skrɪpʃən) *n.* 藥方

After examining me, the doctor gave me a *prescription* to be filled at the drugstore.

【script 是表 write (寫) 的字根】

presentation (ˌprɛzn̩'teʃən) *n.* 報告;敘述

A well-written *presentation* can create a strong impression that will help you a lot in getting a good job.

preserve (prɪ'zɜv) *v.* 保存

In the past, people usually used salt to *preserve* meat and fish.

【serve 是表 keep (保存) 的字根】

presidency ('prɛzədənsı) *n.*
總統的職位；總統的任期

The *presidency* in Taiwan is four years.
【先背 president (總統)】

press conference *n.* 記者會

The movie star held a *press conference* to
announce his retirement.【press 當名詞用
時，可作「新聞記者；新聞」解】

press release *n.* 發表新聞

The president announced his retirement
in a *press release*.

primary ('praɪ,mɛrɪ) *adj.* 主要的

Do not lose sight of your
primary objectives.

【「次要的」則是 secondary 】

prim	+	ary
first	+	adj.

principal (ˈprɪnsəpl̩) *n.* 校長

adj. 主要的

The *principal* reason Clark wants to study abroad is to improve his language skills.【此字與 principle（原則）的發音相同】

principle (ˈprɪnsəpl̩) *n.* 原則

Equality is one of the basic *principles* of democracy.

priority (praɪˈɔrətɪ) *n.* 優先權

Families with a low income will be given *priority*.【*priority seat* 則是「博愛座」】

private (ˈpraɪvɪt) *adj.* 私人的

This is my *private* room.

【相反詞是 public（公共的）】

probationary ﹝ proˈbeʃənˌɛrɪ ﹞ adj.
試用期間的；實習中的

Sherry was hired as a *probationary*
teacher, but after six months she was
offered a permanent position by the
school.

prob	+ at(e)	+ ion	+ ary
prove +	v. +	n. +	adj.

procedure ﹝ prəˈsidʒɚ ﹞ n. 程序

There is a simple *procedure* for buying
the products online.

pro	+ ced	+ ure
forward +	go +	n.

process ﹝ˈprɑsɛs﹞ n. 過程

The automatic ticket system has
simplified the *process* of buying advance
tickets.

productive 〔 prəˋdʌktɪv 〕 *adj.*
有生產力的

The piece of land near the valley is so
fertile that it has been very *productive* of
fruits and other crops.

professional 〔 prəˋfɛʃənḷ 〕 *adj.* 專業的

When I asked the lawyer about my case,
he gave me his *professional* advice.

【相反詞是 amateur 〔ˋæmə͵tʃʊr 〕 *adj.* 業餘的】

profit 〔ˋprɑfɪt 〕 *n.* 利潤

Although business was slow, we still
made a small *profit*. 【*make a profit* 獲取
利潤；它的相反詞是 loss 〔 lɔs 〕 *n.* 損失】

prohibit 〔 proˋhɪbɪt 〕 *v.* 禁止

They believe that nuclear weapons should
be totally *prohibited*. 【prohibit = forbid】

自我測驗

P

- [ ] participate   _____
- [ ] patronage   _____
- [ ] penalty   _____
- [ ] pension   _____
- [ ] pesticide   _____

- [ ] pile   _____
- [ ] portable   _____
- [ ] postpone   _____
- [ ] potential   _____
- [ ] precedent   _____

- [ ] preserve   _____
- [ ] primary   _____
- [ ] private   _____
- [ ] probationary   _____
- [ ] productive   _____

Check List

1. 壓倒性的　　　o _overwhelming_ g
2. 薪水支票　　　p _____ k
3. 行　人　　　　p _____ n
4. 表　演　　　　p _____ e
5. 說　服　　　　p _____ e

6. 全體出席的　　p _____ y
7. 部　分　　　　p _____ n
8. 郵　資　　　　p _____ e
9. 實際的　　　　p _____ l
10. 比較喜歡　　　p _____ e

11. 報告；敘述　　p _____ n
12. 原　則　　　　p _____ e
13. 優先權　　　　p _____ y
14. 過　程　　　　p _____ s
15. 利　潤　　　　p _____ t

P

projection ﹝ prə'dʒɛkʃən ﹞ *n.* 投射；
突出物

The *projection* of the roof shades the
porch and protects us from the rain as
well.

pro	+ ject	+ ion
forward	+ *throw*	+ *n.*

promotion ﹝ prə'moʃən ﹞ *n.* 升遷

He has been working hard since he came
to this company. I think he deserves a
promotion.【此字也可作「促銷」解】

promptly ﹝'prɑmptlɪ ﹞ *adv.* 迅速地；
準時地

Please arrive *promptly* at eight o'clock.

proper ﹝'prɑpɚ ﹞ *adj.* 適當的

What would be a *proper* gift for my
hostess?【proper = appropriate】

proposal 〔 prə'pozḷ 〕 *n.* 提議

We were against William's *proposal*
because it was impracticable.

pro + pos + al
| | |
before + *put* + *n.*

prorate 〔 pro'ret 〕 *v.* 按比率分配

The dividend is *prorated* according to the
number of shares held. 【先背 rate (比率)】

prosper 〔'prɑspɚ 〕 *v.* 繁榮；興盛

The business did not *prosper* and it soon
closed. 【 prosper = flourish = thrive 】

protagonist 〔 pro'tægənɪst 〕 *n.* 主角

The *protagonist* of the novel is a kind of
rebellious anti-hero.

prot + agonist
| |
first + *actor*

provision〔 prə'vɪʒən 〕 *n.* 供給；規定

A *provision* in the contract let us keep pets.【動詞是 provide（提供；規定）】

publication〔 ˌpʌblɪ'keʃən 〕 *n.* 出版；發表

Harry Potter fans eagerly await the *publication* of the seventh book in the series.【先背 public（公開的）】

punctuality〔 ˌpʌnktʃu'ælətɪ 〕 *n.* 守時

Punctuality is not emphasized in South America.

punct + ual + ity
| | |
prick + *adj.* + *n.*

purser〔 'pɝsə 〕 *n.*（輪船、飛機上的）事務長

The captain blamed all of the problems on the *purser*.【先背 purse（錢包）】

Q q

qualification ﹝͵kwɑləfə'keʃən﹞ *n.*
資格

We decided to hire the applicant because
he has the right *qualifications* for the job.

【動詞是 qualify ﹝'kwɑlə͵faɪ﹞ *v.* 使有資格】

quarter ﹝'kwɔrtɚ﹞ *n.* 四分之一；一季

Our profits in the second *quarter* are
only slightly better than those of the
first.

query ﹝'kwɪrɪ﹞ *n.* 詢問【注意發音】

Jonathan's *query* aroused his partner's
suspicion.

questionnaire ﹝͵kwɛstʃən'ɛr﹞ *n.* 問卷

To fill out the *questionnaire* took half an
hour.【先背 question（問題）】

R r

ramp〔 ræmp 〕*n.* 坡道；交流道

Steven drove the car down the *ramp* to his house.

ranch hand　*n.* 牧場工人

Ken is a *ranch hand*, so he can manage a farm very well. 【*ranch hand* = rancher】

range〔 rendʒ 〕*n.* 範圍

I usually score within a *range* of 80 to 90 points on the weekly test.

【range 也可當動詞，如：*range from* A *to* B （範圍）從 A 到 B 都有】

rarely〔ˈrɛrlɪ〕*adv.* 很少

I *rarely* swim in the winter because it is too cold. 【相反詞是 frequently（經常）】

reap〔rip〕v. 收割；獲得回報

Autumn is the time to *reap* rewards for summer's hard work.

rear〔rɪr〕v. 養育 n. 後面；後部

His parents were killed in a car accident and his grandparents *reared* him.

【rear = raise = ***bring up***】

R

reassure〔͵riə'ʃʊr〕v. 使安心

The flight attendant *reassured* the worried passengers that there was nothing wrong with the plane.【先背 assure（向～保證）】

rebate〔rɪ'bet〕v. 退（款）；予以折扣

The store *rebated* one hundred dollars to Amy.【rebate 也可當名詞，如：***a tax rebate***（退稅）】

re	+	bate
again	+	*beat down*（使降價）

receipt 〔 rɪ'sit 〕 *n.* 收據【注意發音】

Be sure to ask for a *receipt* whenever you buy something. 【動詞是 receive (收到)】

receivable 〔 rɪ'sivəbḷ 〕 *adj.* 應受支付的

We do not have much cash on hand because we are still awaiting payment of the accounts *receivable*.

【*accounts receivable* 應收帳款】

receptionist 〔 rɪ'sɛpʃənɪst 〕 *n.* 接待員

Sometimes a medical secretary working for a doctor also acts as a *receptionist*.

【reception 是作「接待；歡迎 (會)」解】

recession 〔 rɪ'sɛʃən 〕 *n.* 不景氣

A large number of people are out of work because of the *recession*. 【recession = depression 】

re	+ cess	+ ion
back+	go	+ *n.*

recommend〔ˌrɛkəˈmɛnd〕v. 推薦

My travel agent *recommended* this hotel.

【recommend = re + commend（稱讚）】

recommendation〔ˌrɛkəmɛnˈdeʃən〕
n. 推薦；推薦信

I didn't know what to order, so I asked the waiter for a *recommendation*.

R

recovery〔rɪˈkʌvərɪ〕n. 恢復；尋回

We were pleased by the *recovery* of the stolen jewels.【先背 cover（覆蓋）】

recreation〔ˌrɛkrɪˈeʃən〕n. 娛樂

It is important to set aside some time for *recreation*, even when you are very busy.

【recreation = re (*again*) + creation（創造）；
recreation = amusement = entertainment】

recruit〔rɪˈkrut〕 *v.* 招募

The Red Lions, Taipei's premier soccer
team, is now *recruiting*
new players.

re	+ cruit
|	|
again +	*grow*

recruitment〔rɪˈkrutmənt〕 *n.* 招募

The government wanted to end the
recruitment of soldiers.

recurrent〔rɪˈkɝənt〕 *adj.* 頻頻發生的

Students making careless mistakes on the
test is a *recurrent* problem.

【可先記住 current
（現在的；在流通的）】

re	+ curr	+ ent
|	|	|
again +	*run* +	*adj.*

recycle〔riˈsaɪkl̩〕 *v.* 回收

Some waste materials
can be *recycled* and
used again.

re	+ cycle
|	|
again +	循環

red tape *n.* 官僚作風

There was a great deal of *red tape* when Bob applied for compensation from the government.【以前的官方文件會用 red tape （紅色的帶子）捆綁】

redecorate〔rɪ'dɛkə,ret〕*v.* 重新裝潢

My neighbors are going to *redecorate* their house.

【redecorate = re (*again*) + decorate （裝潢）】

reduce〔rɪ'djus〕*v.* 減少

Garbage has become a serious problem. We should *reduce* the number of plastic bags used.

re	+ duce
|	|
back	+ *lead*

reference〔'rɛfərəns〕*n.* 參考

There are several books on English grammar available for your *reference*.

【動詞是 refer〔rɪ'fɝ〕*v.* 參考；提到】

reform ﹝ rɪ'fɔrm ﹞ *v.* 改革

The government has promised to *reform* the education system so that students can learn more.【reform = re + form（形成）】

refreshment ﹝ rɪ'frɛʃmənt ﹞ *n.* 提神之物;茶點

There are plenty of *refreshments* at this conference.【動詞是 refresh（使提神）】

refund ﹝ 'ri,fʌnd ﹞ *n.* 退錢
﹝ rɪ'fʌnd ﹞ *v.* 退（錢）

Melvin took the clothing back to the store and tried to get a *refund*, but they refused to give him his money back.
【refund = re (*back*) + fund（資金;基金）】

regain ﹝ rɪ'gen ﹞ *v.* 恢復

She is slowly *regaining* her health.
【regain = re (*again*) + gain（獲得）】

regional (ˈridʒənl̩) *adj.* 區域性的

Regional cooperation is becoming more
and more important in this era.

【「全國性的」則是 national 】

regularly (ˈrɛgjələ‧lı) *adv.* 定期地

We should have our teeth checked by a
dentist *regularly*.

【相反詞是 irregularly (不定期地)】

R

reimbursement (ˌriɪm'bɝsmənt) *n.*
償還

Esther did not keep her receipts, so she
could not receive *reimbursement* for her
travel expenses.

re	+ im	+ burse	+ ment
back	+ in	+ purse	+ n.

related (rɪ'letɪd) *adj.* 有關聯的

The two problems are *related* to each
other. 【*be related to* 與…有關 】

relative ('rɛlətɪv) *n.* 親戚   *adj.* 相關的

My grandmother is the *relative* I like to visit most.

relatively ('rɛlətɪvlɪ) *adv.* 相對地

For a college student, sports are *relatively* unimportant when compared with studying.

reliable (rɪ'laɪəbl̩) *adj.* 可靠的

I want to buy a *reliable* car so that I don't have to spend a lot of money on repairs.

【reliable = dependable = trustworthy；

動詞是 rely（依賴；依靠）】

relief (rɪ'lif) *n.* 放心；鬆了一口氣

We all felt a sense of *relief* after the big exam.

re	+	lief
again	+	*lift*

relieve 〔 rɪ'liv 〕 *v.* 減輕

The nurse gave me some medication to *relieve* the pain.

reluctant 〔 rɪ'lʌktənt 〕 *adj.* 不情願的

Although Tammy was *reluctant* to take the swimming class, she did anyway.

【相反詞是 willing（願意的）】

re	+	luct	+	ant
|		|		|
against	+	*struggle*	+	*adj.*

R

remark 〔 rɪ'mark 〕 *n.* 評論；話

Dennis made an unkind *remark* about Ellen's dress. **【*make a remark* 評論】**

remarkable 〔 rɪ'markəbḷ 〕 *adj.* 驚人的

Considering her age, it is *remarkable* how talented she is.

remit〔rɪˋmɪt〕v. 匯（款）

Please *remit* the money by the end of
May.【remitter 是「匯款人」，
remittee 則是「受款人」】

re	+	mit
back	+	send

remodel〔riˋmɑdḷ〕v. 改造

Natasha is trying to *remodel* her house.
【remodel = re (*again*) + model（塑造）】

remotely〔rɪˋmotlɪ〕*adv.* 遙遠地；
微微地

Nina and Peter have the same
grandfather, but they look only *remotely*
alike.【*remote control* 是指「遙控器」】

renovate〔ˋrɛnəˏvet〕v. 整修；翻新

After buying the old
house, they decided to
completely *renovate* it.

re	+ nov	+ ate
again	+ new	+ v.

【不要與 innovate（創新）搞混】

- [ ] promotion _____
- [ ] prorate _____
- [ ] purser _____
- [ ] quarter _____
- [ ] range _____

- [ ] rebate _____
- [ ] recession _____
- [ ] recreation _____
- [ ] recruit _____
- [ ] reference _____

- [ ] refund _____
- [ ] regional _____
- [ ] reliable _____
- [ ] relieve _____
- [ ] remit _____

R

Check List

1. 適當的   p __*proper*__ r
2. 提　議   p _____ l
3. 出版；發表   p _____ n
4. 資　格   q _____ n
5. 很　少   r _____ y

6. 使安心   r _____ e
7. 收　據   r _____ t
8. 推　薦   r _____ d
9. 回　收   r _____ e
10. 減　少   r _____ e

11. 恢　復   r _____ n
12. 償　還   r _____ t
13. 相對地   r _____ y
14. 評論；話   r _____ k
15. 改　造   r _____ l

R

renowned ﹝ rɪˋnaʊnd ﹞ *adj.* 有名的

A *renowned* scientist was invited to
deliver a lecture at our school.

【renowned = famous = well-known】

rental ﹝ˋrɛntḷ﹞ *n.* 租金 *adj.* 出租的

The monthly *rental* of this studio is two
thousand dollars. 【「租約」是 lease﹝lis﹞】

repetitive ﹝ rɪˋpɛtɪtɪv ﹞ *adj.* 重複的；
囉嗦的

We all felt bored with Monica's *repetitive*
conversation. 【動詞是 repeat（重複）】

replicate ﹝ˋrɛplɪ͵ket﹞ *v.* 複製

The Mona Lisa is a painting that has
been *replicated* countless times.

【replica 是作「複製品」解】

re	+ plic	+ ate
|	|	|
back	+ *fold*	+ *v.*

representative 〔ˌrɛprɪˈzɛntətɪv 〕 *n.*
代表

The chairman sent a *representative* to the
meeting because he was unable to attend.
【可先背 present 〔ˈprɛznt 〕 *adj.* 出席的】

repulse 〔 rɪˈpʌls 〕 *v.* 擊退

I was instantly *repulsed* by his slimy,
unctuous manner.【先背 pulse（脈搏）】

reputation 〔ˌrɛpjəˈteʃən 〕 *n.* 名聲

He enjoys an excellent *reputation* as a
scholar.

requirement 〔 rɪˈkwaɪrmənt 〕 *n.*
要求；必備條件

Concentration is the first *requirement* for
learning.【動詞是 require（需要）】

requisite ('rɛkwəzɪt) *adj.* 必要的；
必備的

Peggy has the *requisite* passion for being
a nanny.

requite (rɪ'kwaɪt) *v.* 回報

Confucius thought that
we must *requite* evil
with good.

re	+ quite
back +	free

reserve (rɪ'zɜv) *v.* 預訂

I'll call the restaurant and *reserve* a table
for tonight.

reside (rɪ'zaɪd) *v.* 居住

The Jones no longer *reside* in that house;
they have moved overseas.

re	+ side
back +	sit

【如果只是暫時居住某處，
動詞是用 stay；*reside in*
= *live in* = *dwell in* = inhabit 】

resident (ˈrɛzədənt) *n.* 居民

Gary is a *resident* of Geneva.

【resident = dweller = inhabitant】

residential (ˌrɛzəˈdɛnʃəl) *adj.* 住宅的

Around the downtown area, there are *residential* areas with houses and apartments.

R

resource (rɪˈsors) *n.* 資源

Students today have many *resources* available to them, including the Internet and the school library. 【source 是指「來源」】

respect (rɪˈspɛkt) *v. n.* 尊敬

We *respect* our parents very much.

restless (ˈrɛstlɪs) *adj.* 浮躁的; 坐立不安的

Sally is a *restless* person and finds it difficult to sit still for long periods of time. 【restless = rest (休息) + less (沒有)】

restore〔rɪ'stor〕*v.* 恢復

The old building was *restored* to its
original condition and
opened as a museum.

re	+ store
|	|
back +	儲存

restriction〔rɪ'strɪkʃən〕*n.* 限制

Due to the age *restriction*, the child
couldn't enter the theater and watch the
movie.

re +	strict	+ ion
|	|	|
back +	*draw tight* +	*n.*

resume〔rɪ'zum〕*v.* 繼續
〔͵rɛzʊ'me〕*n.* 履歷表

They *resumed* the discussion after a short
break.

retail〔'ritel〕*v. n.* 零售　*adj.* 零售的

Retail prices may vary by fifty percent.

【「批發；批發的」則是 wholesale〔'hol͵sel〕】

retention ﹝rɪ'tɛnʃən﹞ *n.* 保有

Retention of our best students benefits the school.

【動詞是 retain﹝rɪ'ten﹞*v.* 保留】

retire ﹝rɪ'taɪr﹞ *v.* 退休

Mr. Goodman hopes to *retire* early, at the age of fifty.【retire = re + tire（使疲倦）】

retrieve ﹝rɪ'triv﹞ *v.* 取回

To train his dog, Robert threw something far away and asked his dog to *retrieve* the object.

reveal ﹝rɪ'vil﹞ *v.* 洩漏

My best friend told me a secret and I promised not to *reveal* it.

re	+	veal
back	+	*veil*

【相反詞是 conceal﹝kən'sil﹞*v.* 隱藏；隱瞞】

revenue ('rɛvə,nju) *n.* (國家的) 收入

A country's *revenue* comes mostly from
taxes.【相反詞是
expenditure (支出)】

re	+	venue
back	+	come

reverse (rɪ'vɝs) *v.* 使顛倒；使倒退

Looking over his shoulder,
the taxi driver *reversed*
the car down the street.

re	+	verse
back	+	turn

R

revive (rɪ'vaɪv) *v.* 使甦醒；恢復

Smelling salts can *revive* one who has
fainted.【名詞是 revival (甦醒；恢復)】

reward (rɪ'wɔrd) *n.* 報酬；獎賞

When Robert got straight A's, his parents
gave him a new computer game as a
reward.

ribbon ('rɪbən) *n.* 緞帶

Diana has a very cute *ribbon* in her hair.

rigger (ˈrɪgɚ) *n.* 索具裝置者

The *rigger* prepared the boat for the journey down the river.【rig 作「索具」解】

round-trip (ˈraʊndˈtrɪp) *adj.* 來回的

David had a *round-trip* ticket to Japan, but he lost it.【*round-trip ticket* 來回票；「單程票」則是 *one-way ticket*；如果把此字拆開，*round trip* 是作「來回旅行」解】

route (rut) *n.* 路線

There are several stops along this bus *route*.【route = way = course】

routine (ruˈtin) *n.* 例行公事；慣例

Ted decided to change his *routine* and take a walk after dinner rather than watch TV.

rug (rʌg) *n.* (小塊) 地毯

The dog prefers to lie on the *rug* rather than the cold floor.【carpet 是作「(整片) 地毯」解】

rumination 〔͵rumə'neʃən〕 *n.* 反芻

When animals re-chew the food in their stomach, we call this *rumination*.

【此字源自 rumen 〔'rumɪn〕 *n.* 瘤胃（反芻動物的第一胃）】

rural 〔'rʊrəl〕 *adj.* 鄉村的

There is not much traffic on these *rural* roads.【相反詞是 urban 〔'ɝbən〕 *adj.* 都市的】

S

rusted 〔'rʌstɪd〕 *adj.* 生銹的

This bicycle is *rusted*.

S s

sabotage 〔'sæbə͵taʒ〕 *n.* 蓄意破壞

The teacher found Sam's act of *sabotage*. He had torn Betty's doll.【此字源自 sabot 〔'sæbo〕 *n.* 木鞋，把木鞋扔進機器裡進行破壞】

sacrifice ('sækrə,faɪs) v. 犧牲

Joe had to *sacrifice* much of his free time
in order to get the
work done on time.

sacri	+	fice
sacred	+	make

safeguard ('sef,gɑrd) v. 保護

Please *safeguard* this treasure while I'm
gone.【safeguard = safe + guard (守護)】

sanitation (,sænə'teʃən) n. 衛生

The mayor has promised to hire more
street cleaners to improve the *sanitation*
of the streets.

sanit	+	ation
healthy	+	n.

scarcely ('skɛrslɪ) adv. 幾乎不

My sister *scarcely* knows how to turn on
a computer let alone program one.
【scarcely = hardly = barely】

schedule (ˈskɛdʒul) *n.* 時間表

I have to check my *schedule*.

scuba diving *n.* 水肺潛水

Scuba diving is getting more and more popular.【scuba（水肺）是由 *self-contained underwater breathing apparatus* 省略而來；diving 在此指「潛水」，也可作「跳水」解】

sealed (sild) *adj.* 密封的

James sent a *sealed* letter to his parents. 【動詞是 seal（密封）】

seasonable (ˈsiznəbl̩) *adj.* 合時宜的

"Jingle Bells" is a *seasonable* song that is often sung on Christmas Eve.

seating (ˈsitɪŋ) *n.* 座位；容納

This theater has a *seating* capacity of five thousand.【seating 是集合名詞】

S

sediment (ˈsɛdəmənt) *n.* 沈澱物

Ocean *sediments* will become petroleum
eventually.

sedi + ment
| |
sit + *n.*

seemingly (ˈsimɪŋlɪ) *adv.* 似乎

A labyrinth is a confusing and *seemingly*
endless array of passages.

【先背 seem (sim) *v.* 似乎】

segment (ˈsɛgmənt) *n.* 部分

The *segment* of the film Jackie missed
turned out to be the most important part.

【相反詞是 whole (hol) *n.* 全部】

selection (səˈlɛkʃən) *n.* 選擇

After browsing in the bookstore for an
hour, Cindy finally made a *selection*.

self-insured (ˌsɛlfɪnˈʃʊrd) *adj.* 自保的

The new *self-insured* employer law
contains fifty clauses.

【先背 insure (為…投保)】

semiconductor (ˌsɛməkənˈdʌktɚ) *n.*
半導體

Semiconductors made in Taiwan are of
high quality.

semi + conductor
| |
half + 傳導體

seminar (ˈsɛməˌnɑr) *n.* 研討會

There will be a two-day *seminar* on
global warming this May.

separate (ˈsɛpəˌret) *v.* 使分開；區別

After we *separated* the fighting boys,
they shook hands.

【相反詞是 unite (juˈnaɪt) *v.* 使聯合 】

session ('sɛʃən) n. 開會；開庭

You must remain quiet when
the court is in *session*.

```
sess + ion
  |     |
 sit  +  n.
```

setting ('sɛtɪŋ) n. 背景

A long white beach made a beautiful
setting for their party.

severe (sə'vɪr) adj. 嚴厲的

Because he made a serious mistake, his
father gave him a *severe* punishment.

【severe = strict = stern = harsh 】

shareholder ('ʃɛr,holdə) n. 股東

Isaac is one of the *shareholders* in this
company.【share 可作「股票」解】

sharpen ('ʃɑrpən) v. 使銳利

This knife couldn't cut anything, so Leo
sharpened it with a knife sharpener.

shelter ('ʃɛltɚ) *n.* 避難所；收容所

The Red Cross provided food and *shelter* to the victims of the earthquake.

shel + ter
| |
shield + troop

shift (ʃɪft) *v.* 轉移

We will *shift* our marketing department to the New York office next month.

shipment ('ʃɪpmənt) *n.* 船貨

The clerk said that a new *shipment* of rugs will arrive tomorrow.

shipping ('ʃɪpɪŋ) *n.* 運貨；船運

Shipping is becoming more and more important in this country.

short-haul ('ʃɔrt'hɔl) *adj.* 短程的

The Taipei-Kaohsiung route is considered a *short-haul* flight by most airlines.

【haul 在這裡是作「運輸距離」解】

- [ ] repetitive
- [ ] requirement
- [ ] requisite
- [ ] residential
- [ ] restriction

- [ ] retention
- [ ] revenue
- [ ] routine
- [ ] rusted
- [ ] scarcely

- [ ] seasonable
- [ ] segment
- [ ] seminar
- [ ] session
- [ ] short-haul

S

1. 租金；出租的　r ___*rental*___ l
2. 名　聲　r _____ n
3. 預　訂　r _____ e
4. 居　民　r _____ t
5. 零售；零售的　r _____ l

6. 退　休　r _____ e
7. 報酬；獎賞　r _____ d
8. 來回的　r _____ p
9. 鄉村的　r _____ l
10. 衛　生　s _____ n

11. 密封的　s _____ d
12. 選　擇　s _____ n
13. 使分開；區別　s _____ e
14. 股　東　s _____ r
15. 轉　移　s _____ t

S

shrine ﹝ ʃraɪn ﹞ *n.* 聖殿；殿堂

One can see many small *shrines* to the
Sea Goddess along the coastal highway.

【可先背 shine（發光），中間再加入 r】

sidewalk ﹝ˈsaɪd͵wɔk ﹞ *n.* 人行道

She fell on the icy *sidewalk*.

【 sidewalk = pavement 】

sightseeing ﹝ˈsaɪt͵siɪŋ ﹞ *n.* 觀光

We would like do some *sightseeing* while
we are in Paris. 【 *do sightseeing* 觀光 】

sign ﹝ saɪn ﹞ *v.* 簽（名） *n.* 告示牌

Helen *signed* her name.

significantly ﹝ sɪgˈnɪfəkəntlɪ ﹞ *adv.*
重要地；意義重大地

Significantly, the percentage of
unemployed people is increasing.

signify ('sɪgnə,faɪ) *v.* 表示

Wedding rings *signify* the couple's commitment.

simplify ('sɪmplə,faɪ) *v.* 簡化

Can you *simplify* what you've just said?

【先背 simple (簡單的)】

simulate ('sɪmjə,let)

v. 模擬

This exercise is meant
to *simulate* a mainland
Chinese invasion of Taipei.

```
simul + ate
  |      |
same  +  v.
```

sincere (sɪn'sɪr) *adj.* 真誠的

In this letter, I express my *sincere*
sympathy for your loss.

【sincere = truthful = honest】

sitting duck *n.* 易受攻擊的目標；
容易受騙的人
Walking through the dangerous jungle
without a gun, Clark was a *sitting duck*.

skyscraper〔'skaɪˌskrepɚ〕*n.* 摩天大樓
It is dangerous to jump off a *skyscraper*.
【skyscraper = sky + scrape（刮；擦）+ r】

sleet〔slit〕*n.* 雨雪
Sleet is falling, so please be careful when
you are driving.

slope〔slop〕*n.* 斜坡
Although he is just a beginner, Keith was
able to ski down the *slope* without falling.

soar〔sor〕*v.* 翱翔；（物價）暴漲
Large birds *soar* overhead, searching for
prey.【不要和 roar（吼叫）搞混】

solicit (sə'lɪsɪt) v. 懇求

His attempts to *solicit* help from the other party failed.

soli	+	cit
whole	+	call

solution (sə'luʃən) n. 解決之道

Try as he might, Ned could not find a *solution* to the problem.

【不要與 resolution (決心) 搞混】

sophisticated (sə'fɪstɪˌketɪd) adj. 複雜的

I have no idea how to operate such *sophisticated* equipment.

soph	+ ist	+ ic	+ at(e)	+ ed
wise	+ 人	+ adj.	+ v.	+ adj.

S

souvenir (ˌsuvə'nɪr) n. 紀念品

She brought back lots of little *souvenirs* from Bali for her co-workers.

spacious (ˈspeʃəs) *adj.* 寬敞的

There is enough room in the *spacious* house for several people to live comfortably.【先背 space (空間)】

sparsely (ˈspɑrslɪ) *adv.* 稀疏地

The room was *sparsely* decorated and had a cold atmosphere.
【相反詞是 densely (濃密地)】

spate (spet) *n.* 氾濫；洪水

After the typhoon, the river was in *spate*.

specialize (ˈspɛʃəlˌaɪz) *v.* 專攻

After completing medical school, the doctor decided to *specialize* in heart surgery.【*specialize in* 專攻】

spell (spɛl) *v.* 拼 (字) *n.* 咒語

He *spelled* his name for me.

splendidly ('splɛndɪdlɪ) *adv.* 輝煌地

This hotel has a *splendidly* furnished lobby.

```
splend + id + ly
  |       |     |
shine + adj. + adv.
```

spoil (spɔɪl) *v.* 破壞；腐壞

The party was *spoiled* by the fight between Jack and Peter.

sponsor ('spɑnsɚ) *v.* 贊助   *n.* 贊助者

The sports shoe maker has volunteered to *sponsor* the race.

```
spons + or
  |      |
promise + 人
```

S

spontaneous (spɑn'tenɪəs) *adj.* 自發性的

Walter stood up and made a *spontaneous* speech during the party.

【相反詞是 planned (plænd) *adj.* 計畫好的】

sports complex　*n.* 體育館

There is a *sports complex* downtown.
【complex 的主要意思是「複雜的」，但在這裡是當名詞用，作「綜合設施」解】

spouse〔spaʊz〕*n.* 配偶

Betty and her *spouse* divorced last year.

stabilize〔'stɛbḷ͵aɪz〕*v.* 使穩定

The medical team could not *stabilize* his condition.【形容詞是 stable (穩定的)】

staff〔stæf〕*n.* 全體職員

The executive has a *staff* of four to help him with research.【此字是集合名詞】

stairway〔'stɛr͵we〕*n.* 樓梯

After hearing his mother's call, Oliver walked down the *stairway*.
【stairway = stair (樓梯) + way (路)】

stapler ('steplɚ) *n.* 釘書機

Vivian used a *stapler* to attach the second page to the first one.【staple 是「釘書針」】

state-run ('stet,rʌn) *adj.* 國營的

There are many *state-run* companies in this country.

【state-run = state (國家) + run (經營)】

stationary ('steʃən,ɛrɪ) *adj.* 固定的

If you have a *stationary* bicycle, you can exercise in your own home.

【此字與 stationery (文具) 的發音相同】

```
sta   + tion + ary
 |        |      |
stand +   n.  + adj.
```

statistics (stə'tɪstɪks) *n. pl.* 統計數字

The *statistics* show that the crime rate is increasing.【statistics 也作「統計學」解】

sternly ('stɜnlɪ) *adv.* 嚴厲地

The teacher scolded Paul *sternly*.

stimulate ('stɪmjə͵let) *v.* 刺激

The good smell from
the kitchen *stimulated*
my appetite.

stimul + ate
| |
prick + *v.*

【相反詞是 deaden (使麻木)】

stipulate ('stɪpjə͵let) *v.* 規定

The law *stipulates* every car must have seat
belts for the driver and every passenger.

stock (stɑk) *n.* 股票；存貨

Mr. El bought *stock* in many companies
as an investment.

storage ('storɪdʒ) *n.* 儲藏

We keep the things that we don't use
very often in the *storage* room.

【動詞是 store (儲存)】

strategy〔'strætədʒɪ〕*n.* 策略

Andrew won the chess game because he followed a good *strategy*.【形容詞是 strategic（戰略上的），唸作〔strə'tidʒɪk〕】

streamline〔'strim,laɪn〕*v.* 使成流線型

The swimmers wear tight-fitting swimsuits to *streamline* their bodies.

【streamline = stream（水流）+ line（線）】

stretch〔strɛtʃ〕*v.* 拉長；伸展

Joe *stretched* a rubber band and aimed it at me.

strew〔stru〕*v.* 撒；散播

It is a Japanese custom to *strew* beans to chase ghosts and bad luck out.

【不要和 straw（稻草；吸管）搞混】

strictly ('strɪktlɪ) *adv.* 嚴格地

She wasn't, *strictly* speaking, beautiful in the accepted sense but she was very attractive.

strikingly ('straɪkɪŋlɪ) *adv.* 顯著地

Taipei 101 stands out *strikingly* as a landmark. 【動詞是 strike (使深刻印象)】

stringently ('strɪndʒəntlɪ) *adv.* 嚴格地

To avoid such car crashes, the traffic regulations should be enforced more *stringently*. 【先背 string (細繩；弦)，處於像弦一樣緊繃的狀態，表示「嚴格地」】

submit (səb'mɪt) *v.* 提出

The young author *submitted* his first story to a magazine.

sub	+	mit
under	+	send

subscribe ﹝ səb'skraɪb ﹞ *v.* 訂閱

We *subscribe* to a morning newspaper.

【subscribe（訂閱）、prescribe（開藥方）、
describe（描述）這三個字不要搞混】

subsequent ﹝'sʌbsɪ,kwɛnt ﹞ *adj.*
隨後的

Our teacher always introduces a topic in
one class and then explains it in detail in
the *subsequent* one.【副詞是 subsequently
（後來）；sequent 是作「連續的」解】

sub + sequ + ent
｜　　｜　　｜
near + *follow* + *adj.*

sub + stitut + ion
｜　　｜　　｜
under + *stand* + *n.*

substitution ﹝,sʌbstə'tjuʃən ﹞ *n.* 代替

Our school's *substitution* of an art
program for sports is popular with some
parents.【動詞是 substitute（用…代替）】

suburban〔 sə'bɝbən 〕 *adj.* 郊區的

More and more people move into
suburban areas not far
from major cities.

【名詞是 suburb（郊區）】

sub + urban
| |
near + 都市的

succeed〔 sək'sid 〕 *v.* 成功；繼承

To *succeed* in business, you have to be
diligent.【名詞是 success（成功）】

succinctly〔 sək'sɪŋktlɪ 〕 *adv.* 簡潔地

All department managers must report
their progress *succinctly* to the CEO
before next week.【 succinctly = suc (*under*)
+ cinct (*gird*) + ly (*adv.*)】

suit〔 sut 〕 *v.* 適合 *n.* 西裝；套裝

The dress *suits* you.

suite 〔 swit 〕 *n.* 套房【注意發音】

John stayed the night in the hotel *suite*.

summary 〔'sʌmərɪ 〕 *n.* 摘要

We decided to read one chapter of the book each and provide a *summary* for one another.【先背 sum（總括）】

supervisor 〔,supɚ'vaɪzɚ 〕 *n.* 監督者；管理人；主管

The *supervisor* was responsible for explaining the new regulations to the workers.

```
super + vis + or
  |      |    |
above + see + 人
```

supplier 〔 sə'plaɪɚ 〕 *n.* 供應者

The *supplier* will deliver our order today.

【「製造業者；廠商」是 manufacturer，「生產者」是 producer，「消費者」是 consumer】

surface ('sɝfɪs) *n.* 表面

The desk has a smooth *surface*.

survey (sə've) *v.* 調查;勘查

Surveyors are *surveying* the area in order
to determine the best
route for the new road.

sur	+	vey
over	+	see

suspect (sə'spɛkt) *v.* 懷疑
('sʌspɛkt) *n.* 嫌疑犯

I am not sure who stole the radio, but I
suspect our neighbor's children.

suspend (sə'spɛnd) *v.* 暫停;使停職

Several flights were *suspended* because
of a hurricane.

sus	+	pend
under	+	hang

自我測驗

- [ ] sightseeing _____
- [ ] simulate _____
- [ ] soar _____
- [ ] souvenir _____
- [ ] specialize _____

- [ ] sponsor _____
- [ ] stabilize _____
- [ ] stapler _____
- [ ] stimulate _____
- [ ] strategy _____

- [ ] submit _____
- [ ] substitution _____
- [ ] suburban _____
- [ ] supervisor _____
- [ ] suspend _____

S

✓ Check List

1. 人行道　　　　s ___sidewalk___ k
2. 表　示　　　　s _____ y
3. 摩天大樓　　　s _____ r
4. 解決之道　　　s _____ n
5. 寬敞的　　　　s _____ s

6. 破壞；腐壞　　s _____ l
7. 配　偶　　　　s _____ e
8. 固定的　　　　s _____ y
9. 股票；存貨　　s _____ k
10. 拉長；伸展　　s _____ h

11. 顯著地　　　　s _____ y
12. 訂　閱　　　　s _____ e
13. 成功；繼承　　s _____ d
14. 摘　要　　　　s _____ y
15. 調查；勘查　　s _____ y

suspiciously 〔 səˈspɪʃəslɪ 〕 *adv.*
懷疑地

Not believing Eric's excuse, Tina looked at him *suspiciously*.

sweep 〔 swip 〕 *v.* 掃

My mother *sweeps* the floor every morning.【「掃帚」是 broom】

symbolize 〔ˈsɪmbḷˌaɪz 〕 *v.* 象徵

A dove *symbolizes* peace.
【先背 symbol（象徵）】

S

sympathy 〔ˈsɪmpəθɪ 〕 *n.* 同情

We expressed our *sympathy* to the widow.

sym	+	pathy
together	+	*feeling*

symptom 〔ˈsɪmptəm 〕 *n.* 症狀

The doctor asked Ted about his *symptoms* in order to make a diagnosis.

tab 240 **talented**

T t

tab ﹝ tæb ﹞ *n.* 帳單

Peter lost the bet, so he picked up the *tab*.

【*pick up the tab* 付帳；tab = bill = check】

tablet ﹝'tæblɪt﹞ *n.* 藥片

The *tablet* was so large that I had trouble
swallowing it.【「藥丸」是 pill；「膠囊」是
capsule；「藥粉」是 powder】

take effect 生效

The policy *takes effect* immediately after
you buy it.

talented ﹝'tæləntɪd﹞ *adj.* 有才能的

Ted is the most *talented* pianist we have.
Furthermore, he is very reliable.

【talented = gifted】

tariff (ˈtærɪf) *n.* 關稅

Tariffs are imposed on alcohol and tobacco. 【tariff = duty】

tax break   *n.* 所得稅減免額

You can get a *tax break* by making a donation.【break 的主要意思是「休息」，但在這裡是作「優惠」解】

tear (tɪr) *n.* 眼淚   (tɛr) *v.* 撕裂

He *tore* the envelope open.

【動詞的三態變化為：tear-tore-torn】

technician (tɛkˈnɪʃən) *n.* 技術人員

The *technician* assembled the computer in a systematic way.

【先背 technique (技術)】

teller (ˈtɛlɚ) *n.* 出納員

Ellie works as a *teller* in the bank.

temporarily ('tɛmpə,rɛrəlɪ) *adv.*
暫時地

The workers were dismissed *temporarily* from work.

tempor + ari + ly
| | |
time + *adj.* + *adv.*

tenant ('tɛnənt) *n.* 房客

The *tenants* signed a one-year lease on the apartment.【「房東」是 landlord】

tentative ('tɛntətɪv) *adj.* 暫時的

These plans are *tentative*; we will confirm them later.

tenure ('tɛnjə) *n.* (不動產之) 保有權

In China, there is no *tenure* for life. Residents must rent land from the government.

ten + ure
| |
hold + *n.*

【*tenure for life* 土地終身保有權】

terminal 〔'tɝmənḷ〕

adj. 終點的；末期的

n. 航空站；(公車)總站

```
termin + al
  |       |
limit   + adj.
```

She has *terminal* cancer.

textile 〔'tɛkstḷ〕 *adj.* 紡織的   *n.* 紡織品

Taiwan's *textile* industry is shifting to
Southeast Asia. 【先背 text (內文)，text 是
表 weave (編織) 的字根，文章需要經過編排】

thorough 〔'θɝo〕 *adj.* 徹底的

The police made a *thorough* search for
the escaped criminal, but in vain.

thoughtful 〔'θɔtfəl〕 *adj.* 體貼的

Nancy is a very *thoughtful* person. She
always thinks of the needs of her friends.

【 thoughtful = considerate 】

tie〔 taɪ 〕*v.* 綁;打(結)　　*n.* 領帶

Edward uses a rope to *tie* the boat.

timeline〔'taɪm'laɪn 〕*n.* 時間線

Our history teacher asked us to make a
timeline, placing the events we had
learned about in chronological order.

tolerance〔'tɑlərəns 〕*n.* 容忍;寬容

Nancy is so critical that she has no
tolerance for her employees' mistakes.

【動詞是 tolerate〔'tɑləˌret 〕*v.* 容忍】

toll-free〔ˌtol'fri 〕*adj.* 不必付通行費的

During traditional festival holidays,
highways are *toll-free*.

【toll-free = toll(通行費)+ free(免費的)】

tow〔 to 〕*v.* 拖

Carl's car was *towed* away because he
parked it next to a red line.

track (træk) *n.* 鐵軌

The train left the *tracks*. 【track = rail】

transatlantic (ˌtrænsət'læntɪk) *adj.*
橫越大西洋的

Because the *transatlantic* cable broke, we
can't connect with the
U.S. at the moment.
【「太平洋」是 Pacific】

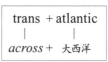

trans	+ atlantic
|	|
across +	大西洋

transfer (træns'fɝ) *v.* 轉移；轉乘；
調職

He was *transferred* from
Taipei to Hong Kong.

trans	+	fer
|		|
across	+	*carry*

transmission (træns'mɪʃən) *n.* 傳送

With a computer, the *transmission* of
images takes only seconds.

【動詞是 transmit (træns'mɪt) *v.* 傳送】

treasury (ˈtrɛʒərɪ) *n.* 國庫

The minister is responsible for the
treasury department of the government.
【先背 treasure (ˈtrɛʒɚ) *n.* 寶藏】

trend (trɛnd) *n.* 趨勢

The *trend* of prices is still upwards.

trepidation (ˌtrɛpəˈdeʃən) *n.* 恐懼

He approached the snake with
trepidation, ready to run should it try to
attack him.

trepid	+ ation
tremble +	*n.*

turbulence (ˈtɝbjələns) *n.* 亂流

We had a bumpy flight due to air
turbulence.【turb 是表「擾亂」的字根，
如 disturb (dɪˈstɝb) *v.* 打擾】

turmoil 〔'tɜmɔɪl 〕 *n.* 騷動；混亂

The city was in *turmoil* after the electricity was cut off.

tutor 〔'tutɚ , 'tjutɚ 〕 *n.* 家庭教師

Doris has her own private *tutor*.

typographical 〔ˌtaɪpə'græfɪkḷ 〕 *adj.*
印刷上的

There are too many *typographical* errors in this manuscript, so its publication will be delayed. 【graph 是表「寫」的字根】

U u

【U/V/W】

unanimous 〔 juˈnænəməs 〕 *adj.*
意見一致的

Scientists are not *unanimous* about the

un	+	anim	+	ous
one	+	mind	+	adj.

reason for the extinction of the dinosaurs.

undergo 〔͵ʌndɚˈgo 〕 *v.* 經歷

All newcomers in this company have to *undergo* some job training.

【undergo = experience = *go through*】

unpack 〔 ʌnˈpæk 〕 *v.* 打開（行李）；
打開並取出（裡面的東西）

I will *unpack* my suitcase as soon as we return.

```
un + pack
 |     |
not + 打包
```

upcoming 〔ˈʌp͵kʌmɪŋ 〕 *adj.*
即將到來的

The *upcoming* class reunion gave her the motivation she needed to finally get in shape.

up-to-date 〔ˈʌptəˈdet 〕 *adj.* 最新的

Do you have an *up-to-date* address for her?【相反詞是 out-of-date（過時的）】

urban (ˈɝbən) *adj.* 都市的

The new park is a wonderful addition to the *urban* environment.

【相反詞是 rural (ˈrurəl) *adj.* 鄉村的】

V v

vacate (ˈveket) *v.* 搬出；辭退（職位）

Rachel had owed her landlord rent for a long time, so she was forced to *vacate* the apartment.

vac + ate
| |
empty + *v.*

valid (ˈvælɪd) *adj.* 有效的

This ticket is *valid* for only two days.

【相反詞是 invalid（無效的）】

venue (ˈvɛnju) *n.* 舉辦地點

This stadium is the best *venue* for a concert.【ven 是表 come（來）的字根】

verify ('vɛrəˌfaɪ) *v.* 證實

It's impossible to *verify* their accounts,
because no physical evidence exists.

【先背 very (眞正的)；verify = prove 】

via ('vaɪə) *prep.* 經由

The parcel arrived *via* the postal service.

【 via = through = by = *by way of* 】

vice-president ('vaɪs'prɛzədənt) *n.*
副總統

Victoria is going to run for *vice-president*.

vigilant ('vɪdʒələnt) *adj.* 警戒的

The guards ought to be *vigilant* at all
times. 【先背 vigil ('vɪdʒəl) *n.* 守夜；看守，
與 visual (視覺的) 的發音相同 】

virtual ('vɝtʃuəl) *adj.* 虛擬的

Virtual computer environments no longer
enjoy the novelty they once did.

visibility 〔ˌvɪzə'bɪlətɪ〕 *n.* 能見度

The airport was closed due to poor *visibility*.【*poor visibility* 能見度低】

volume 〔'vɑljəm〕 *n.* 音量；（書）冊

He turned up the *volume* on the television.

volunteer 〔ˌvɑlən'tɪr〕 *n.* 自願者 *v.* 自願

The charity organization is staffed by *volunteers*.【形容詞是 voluntary（自願的）】

W w

wage 〔wedʒ〕 *n.* 工資

The workers at the factory were paid a *wage* of nine dollars an hour.

【wage 是指按鐘點、天數等計酬的勞動報酬；
  wage = pay = payment】

wake (wek) v. 叫醒

The function of an alarm clock is to *wake* people up at a certain time.

【*wake up* 叫醒 (= *waken* = *awaken*)】

wall-to-wall ('wɔltə'wɔl) adj.
全體的；到處可見的

The *wall-to-wall* corruption in the country makes its government ineffective.

warehouse ('wɛr,haʊs) n. 倉庫

Our *warehouse* is full of cartons of toys.

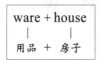

ware + house
|　　　 |
用品 + 房子

warranty ('wɔrəntɪ) n. 保證 (書)

This car's *warranty* lasts for five years.

【warranty = guarantee】

waste〔west〕*n. v.* 浪費

Prior to the use of computers, there was a big *waste* of human resources.

【相反詞是 save〔sev〕*v.* 節省】

wasteful〔'westfəl〕*adj.* 浪費的

Andy used to live in a *wasteful* way, so he spent all his inheritance in a short time.

【相反詞是 economical〔,ikə'nɑmɪkḷ〕*adj.* 節省的】

watchful〔'wɑtʃfəl〕*adj.* 小心的

Be *watchful* for cars when you cross the street.

wheelchair〔'hwil'tʃɛr〕*n.* 輪椅

Donna is a volunteer at the hospital and helps to push patients in *wheelchairs*.

【wheelchair = wheel（輪子）+ chair（椅子）】

willingness 〔'wɪlɪŋnɪs 〕 *n.* 樂意；願意

The singer expressed her *willingness* to
be the spokesperson for the charity drive.

【相反詞是 unwillingness（不樂意；不願意）】

wire 〔 waɪr 〕 *n.* 電線；鐵絲

We had no power after the electrical
wires were cut. 【wireless 是作「無線的」解】

withdraw 〔 wɪθ'drɔ 〕 *v.* 提（款）

Helen *withdrew* money from her account
and went shopping. 【先背 draw（拉）；
「存（錢）」則是 deposit 〔 dɪ'pɑzɪt 〕】

wonder 〔'wʌndɚ 〕 *n.* 奇蹟；奇觀
v. 想知道

It is a *wonder* that he survived the plane
crash. 【不要與 wander（徘徊）搞混，可先
背 wonderful（令人驚嘆的；很棒的）】

wordily ('wɝdɪlɪ) *adv.* 冗長地

The principal always speaks *wordily*, so no one likes to listen to him.

workforce ('wɝk,fɔrs) *n.* 全體工作人員

Some members of the *workforce* will change jobs this summer.

【workforce = work (工作) + force (力量)】

workload ('wɝk,lod) *n.* 工作量

James decided to hire an assistant in order to lessen his own *workload*.

【workload = work (工作) + load (負擔)】

workout ('wɝk,aʊt) *n.* 練習；運動

As the contest is approaching, the school team has a *workout* every day.

【「練習；運動」的片語就是 *work out*】

自我測驗

- [ ] symptom　　　_____
- [ ] take effect　　_____
- [ ] tariff　　　　_____
- [ ] temporarily　　_____
- [ ] terminal　　　_____

- [ ] toll-free　　　_____
- [ ] transfer　　　_____
- [ ] turbulence　　_____
- [ ] unanimous　　_____
- [ ] upcoming　　　_____

- [ ] urban　　　　_____
- [ ] via　　　　　_____
- [ ] warranty　　　_____
- [ ] wonder　　　_____
- [ ] wordily　　　_____

W

Check List

1. 同　情　　　　s _sympathy_ y
2. 有才能的　　　t _____ d
3. 技術人員　　　t _____ n
4. 房　客　　　　t _____ t
5. 徹底的　　　　t _____ h

6. 容忍；寬容　　t _____ e
7. 傳　送　　　　t _____ n
8. 趨　勢　　　　t _____ d
9. 騷動；混亂　　t _____ l
10. 最新的　　　　u _____ e

11. 有效的　　　　v _____ d
12. 舉辦地點　　　v _____ e
13. 倉　庫　　　　w _____ e
14. 提（款）　　　w _____ w
15. 工作量　　　　w _____ d

W

TOEIC 測驗簡介

【聽力測驗】

考試型態	說　　　　明	題數	時間
照片敘述	看到測驗本上的圖片,並聽到四個描述圖片內容的句子,選出正確的句子	10	45分
應答問題	聽到一句問句,並聽到三句回答句,選出正確的句子	30	
簡短對話	聽到兩個人的對話,選出正確的回答句	30	
簡短獨白	聽到一段敘述,選出正確的回答句	30	

【閱讀測驗】

考試型態	說　　　　明	題數	時間
單句填空	選出正確的單字填空,以完成句子	40	75分
短文填空	選出正確的單字填空,以完成短文	12	
單篇文章理解	閱讀一篇文章後,選出正確的回答句	28	
雙篇文章理解	閱讀相關的雙篇文章後,選出正確的回答句	20	

TOEIC 評分標準：最低 10 分，滿分 990 分

分　　數	證　書　顏　色
860 - 990	金　色
730 - 855	藍　色
470 - 725	綠　色
220 - 465	棕　色
10 - 215	橘　色

台灣地區各級學歷 TOEIC 測驗平均分數

教育程度	考試人數	聽力測驗	閱讀測驗	平均總分
語言學校/語言中心	234	340	282	623
碩士以上	28,644	315	285	600
一般大學	61,376	313	264	577
科技大學/技術學院	27,940	249	180	429
專科學校	6,990	246	184	430
高中職業學校	3,473	257	192	449
普通高中	9,823	319	261	580
國　　中	676	307	214	521
國　　小	290	314	266	580

【口說測驗】測驗時間約 20 分鐘

考試型態	說　　明	題數	準備時間	作答時間
朗　讀	朗讀一段英文短文	2	45 秒	45 秒
描述照片	描述螢幕上的照片內容	1	30 秒	45 秒
回答問題	依據題目設定的情境，回答與日常生活有關的問題	3	無	15 秒/30 秒
依據題目資料應答	依據題目設定的情境與提供的資料回答問題	3	無	15 秒/30 秒
提出解決方案	依據題目設定的情境，針對問題點提出對策或解決方案	1	30 秒	60 秒
陳述意見	針對指定的議題陳述意見並提出理由	1	15 秒	60 秒

【寫作測驗】測驗時間約 60 分鐘

考試型態	說　　明	題數	作答時間
描述照片	使用兩個指定單字或片語，造出與照片內容相符的句子	5	共 8 分鐘
回覆書面要求	閱讀 25～50 字的電子郵件後撰寫回信	2	每題10 分鐘
陳述意見	針對指定的議題陳述意見並提出理由及例子作為佐證	1	30 分鐘

TOEIC 口説測驗評分標準

　　前四個題型採 0～3 分的評分級距，後兩個題型採 0～5 分的評分級距。之後再透過統計程序，將各大題的得分換算爲 0～200 分。這 0～200 分又對應到八個能力等級，其對應關係如下：

分　　數	等　級
190-200	8
160-180	7
130-150	6
110-120	5

分　　數	等　級
80-100	4
60-70	3
40-50	2
0-30	1

TOEIC 寫作測驗評分標準

　　第一個題型採 0～3 分的評分級距，第二個題型採 0～4 分的評分級距，第三個題型採 0～5 分的評分級距。之後再透過統計程序，將各大題的得分換算爲 0～200 分。這 0～200 分又對應到九個能力等級，其對應關係如下：

分　　數	等　級
200	9
170-190	8
140-160	7
110-130	6
90-100	5

分　　數	等　級
70-80	4
50-60	3
40	2
0-30	1

NEW TOEIC 常考字彙
【創新錄音版】

附錄音 QR 碼　售價：190 元

主　　編／劉　毅

發　行　所／學習出版有限公司

　　　　　　TEL (02) 2704-5525

郵 撥 帳 號／05127272 學習出版社帳戶

登　記　證／局版台業 2179 號

印　刷　所／裕強彩色印刷有限公司

台 北 門 市／台北市許昌街 17 號 6F

　　　　　　TEL (02) 2331-4060

台灣總經銷／紅螞蟻圖書有限公司

　　　　　　TEL (02) 2795-3656

本公司網址／www.learnbook.com.tw

電 子 郵 件／learnbook0928@gmail.com

2024 年 3 月 1 日新修訂

ISBN 978-986-231-474-6